Heaven's Power

Visit http://www.montrebible.com

First edition, December 2011

© 2011 Montre Bible. All rights reserved.

ISBN 978-1-105-36036-7

Cover photo by
Robert Kneschke/istockphoto.com

"For we wrestle not against flesh and blood, but against principalities, **against powers**, against the rulers of the darkness of this world"

Ephesians 6:12

Heaven's Power

Power

Book Four of the Heaven Sent Series

By Montré Bible

Heaven Sent Series: Book IV

CHAPTER ONE

"**W**hat are you doing Andrew?" Jason, my Latino buddy here in college peeked over my shoulder. He always just let himself into my apartment like it was his. I was over at the computer concentrating so hard at the screen I hadn't heard him come in and make himself a sandwich.

"Oh, um, I'm googling on someone." Doing Google searches on people's names was the best way to find out little tidbits about people and the girl I was dating had a dark history. But it wasn't her name I was doing a search on.

"I hope you're not googling me," Jason said walking over to spy over my shoulder.

"No, I'm doing a Google on Amy's teacher."

"Amy's teacher? You mean the one that violated her? Andrew, why are you meddling?"

"I'm not meddling."

"Yes, you are. She said she wanted to forget. Don't you think you should leave well enough alone?" That's easier said than done. Maybe I was meddling just a tad but there was a reason that my powers kept showing me visions about her life and I had to do something about it. That's right, I said powers. I have supernatural abilities that run in my family that allow me to just see into people's lives just by touching them or being close to them. I'm told it's called being an empath but that's not the only thing different about me, or my family. But I knew I didn't just have these abilities for no reason.

I shook my head. "I keep thinking back about how she told me that she didn't think God cared about her."

"Why would she say something like

that," Jason asked sitting on the floor and resting his back against the wall.

"Because she said she would pray and pray about that situation and nothing ever happened."

"But she never told anyone either."

"Well she told me."

"So what are you going to do, Andrew? Play God and try to answer her prayer now?" Jason's slight accent seemed to only intensify his sarcasm.

"No I'm not playing God, Jason. I'm just going to be, let's say, God's little angel." It was more than a pun. What made my family so different was that I actually had angel blood in my veins. My grandfather, Donyel, is a fallen angel but that was the least of my worries at the moment.

"I'm sure the angels are doing the best job they can; they don't need your help," Jason pointed out somewhat defensively.

"Well, I'm not trying to help the angels. I'm trying to help a friend."

"By meddling."

"I'm not meddling," I snapped back still scrolling the screen for some bit of information to give me something on her teacher's whereabouts. "Hmm, background checks."

"So," Jason continued, "what are you going to do when you find this guy? You going to question him? You going to go beat him up?"

I stopped to glance at Jason. "No, I haven't thought that far ahead. And if I were thinking that way, I would do better to get Antonio to beat him up." Antonio, my twin brother had supernatural strength and speed. I felt he was a pretty good fall back plan if I ever got in jam. Sometimes I think even without his powers he would still be stronger than me.

"True."

"You didn't have to agree so fast," I cleared my throat.

"Sorry." He stuffed another bite of a sandwich into his mouth.

"Why do you think that some prayers go unanswered, Jason?"

He thought for a second and wiped his mouth, "Prayers are living once you speak them and they have to travel through the heavens kind of like radio signals" He gestured heaven above his head, "The Bible says in several scriptures if you trust him he will hear your prayer but that also prayers can be hindered by how you treat others here on earth."

"But what has she done to anybody? And if she feels the way she does then she has a right. Look at what happened to her."

"But you can't send a hate prayer, I'm sure. But I also said that prayers have to travel and that if you trust and have faith, God will hear it. The opposite of that would be fear and doubt." Jason said trying to make his point. It reminded me of our discussions after campus Bible study, "I imagine that the angels have to take the prayers to God, like mailmen."

"Are you saying angels are like UPS now?"

"Better example, like football players." I turned my chair when he said this and looked like a lost puppy. "Come Andrew, stick with me, think of it like this. A prayer goes into play and a team of angels have to get that one prayer to God. What hinders that prayer is the opposite team and what they represent, like fear and doubt. So they will either try to intercept the prayer or make it fumble."

"So praying is spiritual sport? That sucks, cause it means that the likelihood of a prayer being hindered is high."

"Not necessarily, because if we are

continually rooting for our team and keeping their spirits up they will win." Jason sung a "we got spirit" cheer and kicked his leg up.

"Uh, don't do that in my living room. But I get your point, you're saying that our faith and our praise to God…"

"…empowers the angels to perform better and thus get our prayers through to God," Jason interrupted.

"You didn't let me finish."

"Sorry." Jason smiled. "But you like my illustration?"

"Yeah, makes me visualize what might be going on in the spiritual realm. It's weird how there's so much that we do in this world that could be related on how the spirit world works."

"I think that this world we live in is just a reflection of the supernatural world we can't see," Jason said putting his plate up.

"How did you get so deep into spiritual

and supernatural stuff, Jason?"

"Same as you, my father got me into it. Have you had any luck on your search yet?" I turned back around to my screen and looked and the people search website. I gathered a few names and did a cross reference on the town of Galatia.

"Got him!" I looked at the screen, "Mr. Cornelius Garrett. Lived in Galatia, Texas for about ten years and now lives in Houston."

"That's only five hours away, you ready to go beat him up?"

I gave a Jason a mean glare and continued reading. "Oh no."

"What?"

"Oh man, what could this mean?" I sat stunned for a moment at the information I was reading on the screen.

"What's wrong," Jason asked.

I looked at Jason and rubbed the back of

my bald head. "Nothing, I think I'm getting charged for this information." I sort of lied, God forgive me. But I didn't want to involve him anymore than I had to. Besides, everything was coming full circle and he wouldn't understand that what bothered me the most about what I saw on the screen was that Mr. Cornelius Garrett was born in Heaven, Texas. Heaven Texas was where I was from and my little town had a bad notorious habit of producing a few devils and angels here on earth.

"So where's your brother?"

"Antonio?" I asked as if I had another brother to choose from. "Oh he's out practicing basketball as usual. I'm surprised you're not off campus already since school has been out. Are you going to spend the winter holidays with your family?"

Jason shook his head. "I have a major assignment I have to finish before I can go home.

I don't want to get behind that's why I'm still here."

"Dang Jason, that's being a workaholic or a school-aholic or whatever you would call it. I mean it's the holidays and you should be with your family," I said trying to help him see the error of his ways. I for one was not that interested in school to be spending my every waking hour studying. It just wasn't that serious.

"I talked to my family, but I live too far to be going back and forth and I really need to finish this project. My father wouldn't have it any other way. He sent me here and he knows what I have to do, he supports me 100% as long as I'm not here goofing off."

"Sounds like you have a really strict family," I laughed.

"Probably no more strict than your dad is about a lot of things." My dad, Anthony, was not only very educated on all things biblical or spiritual but he took life very seriously. Because my grandfather was a fallen angel, Anthony was very paranoid about demon attacks or anything out of the ordinary trying to hurt me or my brother Antonio because we were part angel or what some called part nephilim. We had already lost my mother, Andrea—a half breed, a few years ago because of spiritual causes and my dad was just being cautious. Or at least that's how I saw it.

"Point taken." I couldn't imagine being on campus studying on December 25th when everyone else was singing Christmas carols and watching reruns of "It's a wonderful life" so I did what any good friend would do.

"Hey Jason, why don't you grab your books and spend Christmas with my family."

"Ah man," Jason scratched his head, "I don't want to impose on your family."

"Impose? Man you're always in my

apartment anyhow." I put my hands on his shoulders, "It would be weird for me to be opening up gifts thinking you were still here on campus with your nose in a book."

"Andrew, I…"

I stuck my hand up. "Jason, I'm not taking no for an answer. You're coming, that way I don't have to worry about your mother worrying about you being lonely."

"Thanks, Andrew. That's really cool of you."

I smiled and patted Jason on the back. "Don't mention it. I'll call my dad and let him know you're coming. We're going to make this a holiday to remember."

Jason smirked and nodded. "I believe it will be."

CHAPTER TWO

"I found it," Tamela Jeffries said holding a small box. She sat on the floor inside her garage and laid it on her lap. Tamela was known to study witchcraft and own a store of the magickal arts under the guise of a bookstore in Heaven, Texas. Small town folk didn't take kindly to her. They just didn't bother with her at all mainly out of fear but she managed to survive by selling a few love spells to young girls and palm reading disgruntled wive's lives secretly. She was like a drug dealer of all things spiritual. What people didn't know was that she was communicating to Donyel and planned on releasing him from a spiritual prison that Andrea had locked him in years ago.

A little cat slithered next to her and

scratched at the box. "*Open it, this is what we're looking for,*" It telepathically said to her. It was possessed with the dead spirit of this guy named Philip. Philip was Donyel's half-breed son and Andrea's brother. Being brought back in this cat's body was his "reward" or his hell, depends on how you look at it.

She popped the lock with a small key and slowly opened the lid revealing the contents. She took in her hands papers with all types of old spells written on them and small vials filled with mysteriously colored liquids. But that wasn't what she was looking for. She rummaged through it until she found a braided lock of hair. She raised it up and smiled. "Andrea's hair."

"*Andrea's essence; it's just as much a part of her as anything else. We don't have her but some of her power is in that. It should be enough to do what we have to do.*" The little cat sat so still like a statue. Tamela felt eerie that her ex-boyfriend's spirit possessed that creature. It was unbelievable and she knew she should've been scared but after Donyel had come into her life she knew that anything could happen. Her own personal angel had come into her life to grant her wisdom and power when she was in college and that had been taken away from her. Her daughter, Tonya, had been taken away from her and now this was a miracle. All things were possible in her view. It hurt to see her beautiful daughter laying in the hospital as a vegetable. The doctors said that Tonya's mind was simply gone. Her angel would restore her daughter. Donyel would do this for her, because he was her guardian, she believed that.

"It's all Andrea's sons' fault that my daughter is like she is. But Donyel has the power to make her whole again. I have faith in him. It's been so long, where is the old plantation house located?" The old plantation house is where

Donyel was trapped. But it had imploded in a fiery gulf when Andrea had last confronted him and locked him in nether region of existence.

"I will take you there," Philip said to her. She packed the things she had used to conjure Donyel the first time and placed the hair in a plastic bag and safely between her cleavage.

It was a cold breezy night when she got to the all familiar woods on the outskirts of the town. She kept a flashlight in one hand and followed the little cat, who only stopped periodically to not lose her, *"Quickly, time is wasting,"* Philip said to her.

Tamela pulled her jacket tighter around her neck and double-timed her paced to keep up. Leaves blew everywhere and the sounds of the wild startled her at times. She was nervous of running into a bobcat or a javelina that were known to attack if provoked. Her satchel was strapped closely to her side. There was a break in the woods, and finally a large field where no grass grew. The dirt was dry and lifeless. The cat sat in one spot looking up into the sky with its' back to her.

"This is the spot."

"It's too windy," Tamela explained, "I won't be able to keep the candles lit." The cat bowed and its' eyes glowed but Tamela wasn't sure if it was because of the flashlight's glare or were they actually glowing. The wind grew wilder and diverted into a cyclone around them creating an eye of peace where they stood. Tamela dropped to her knees in awe. Somehow they were untouched by the effects of the breeze but everything around them continued to be disturbed.

"Do the incantation now," Philip commanded Tamela. She took the candles out the satchel and wedged them into a circle in the dirt and lit them. She took Andrea's hair and

pulled out the paper to conjure Donyel.

"Angel spirit over me, come from your hiding place, may your presence now be in my realm face to face." She said that three times and burnt the paper along with the hair letting the ashes fall within the circle. The candles flickered out and her heart jumped knowing that something was happening and it had to do with Donyel. The cat jerked around facing the circle she had made with anticipation. A long minute had transgressed.

"Did I do it right? Nothing's happening," Tamela said. Immediately the wind commenced with a powerful gust. Dirt and leaves blew everywhere. The candles relit themselves in hot long torch-like blazes. She screamed. The cat ran to her feet. The candles instantly melted in place but the circular holes that were made from their placement remained glowing like fiery embers. A rolling sound of the ground breaking open warned Tamela to step aside. It reminded her of the sound when she accidentally ground a chicken bone in the garbage disposal. She lost her footing as the ground separated beneath her feet. Black smoky clouds emitted from the cracks charged with lightning. Those clouds resembled a snake as they formed and wound around in the air. It charged and struck the ground with bolts of electricity. A victorious echoing laugh came from it. Tamela lost her footing and scooted along the ground in fear trying to avoid the bolts of lightning from hitting her.

"Tamela, my servant!" The cloud wound itself to the ground and shaped instantly into a form of a man. It was Donyel. He was kneeling in a stance like a cat ready to pounce; his long black silky hair draped over his cold alabaster naked skin. He held a coy smirk revealing his pinkish lips which contrasted delightful with pale, androgynous visage. His fiery piercing eyes were locked on Tamela and he stood.

Tamela crawled over to him and kissed his feet. "My Lord. I have released you with a request. My daughter that you have blessed me with is sick. Bring her back to me please."

Donyel tilted his head. "Tonya, yes. This will be done in time. But I, Donyel, am now free!" Donyel raised his head and smiled as to mock something above him. "I am free! And I will get my revenge. You will help me get those who placed me here and after that I will do as you have requested."

Tamela looked pleased. "What is it that you're going to do? Are you going to strike them with your wrath, my Lord?"

Donyel took her by the hand, "My plan is as it always has been. I will get what I want. I am Donyel and I always get what I want." He lifted her to embrace her. Tamela's feet dangled because of his height; she shivered at his beauty. He resembled those men on the cover of romance novels. His arms, his abs, his bare chest were simply perfect. And even though his skin appeared dead and cold it was hot to the touch.

"It's been a long time," he said caressing her lips with his long fingers, "let us begin."

CHAPTER THREE

"I made it safely." I told Amelia on the phone. She hated for me to call her Amelia, she preferred just Amy.

"Good, I'm glad. Thanks for calling me," Amy said. Two nights before Christmas and the house had a lot of activity going on with the Christmas music that Karen had put on and the decorations, it really gave it a whole different feel. Karen and Anthony were just friends in college but now that my mother was dead, things seemed to be changing between them.

"I'm just hanging out with my mom right now and a few family members," Amy said on the phone. I nodded struggling to hear but Karen and my dad were laughing way too hard, I guess they were reminiscing about old college days.

Courtney, Karen's daughter, was there in the house as well talking with Jason. She glanced at me a couple of times but played it off when I looked her direction. Antonio was outside shooting his basketball through my old basketball hoop attached to side of the house.

"I can't wait to see you again." Amy said, "I had a really good time and I got you something for Christmas." Ahh, it gave a warm fuzzy feeling. It wasn't too often that I got a gift from a girl…okay never. Did that mean I needed to get her something? Then again, that could be also signs that she's moving way too fast. I mean really, did a present mean that we were officially dating? I looked at Courtney. As much as I tried to concentrate on Amy, Courtney was always on my mind. There was some connection between us other than she knew about my supernatural abilities and Amy didn't. Why did I always have to be so split?

"I'll be back some time after Christmas, God forbid I spend New Years here, there's absolutely nothing to do," I dryly said. She laughed. Amy was the cat's meow and so easy to talk to. So why was my interest for her so low right now? Courtney had made it plain that she wanted nothing to do with me. I guess that's the downside to not being normal. It was just too much for her to handle. Courtney had made her decision and I needed to let go. Besides, Courtney was dating Leonard Freeman, the one guy in Heaven, Texas that I wished a meteorite would just land on....accidentally of course. If only it was that easy. "I can barely hear, Amy, I'll call you later, okay?"

"Okay, Andrew, have a merry Christmas."

"You too." I hung up the phone and I meshed my way into Jason and Courtney's conversation.

"I think I want to change my major to Art Direction." Courtney told Jason.

He smiled, nodded and acknowledged my presence. "I was just telling Courtney how cool our school is and she should consider transferring." Courtney had gone to school way in California to get away from the craziness of my life and family. Getting attacked by demons just didn't happen to everybody and she wanted a normal life. I understood.

"Um." I thought that Jason was meddling now. "It's not all that great actually," I said.

"Well, I like my school," Courtney confirmed, "I've lived in Dallas all my life and it's good to get away and see how other people live." I wished I could get away right now.

"There's a lot of people here, where are we going to sleep at?" Jason asked. Our bags were still at the door. I was thinking the same question.

"Me-ma said that Karen, Courtney, and one other person can stay at her house." Anthony said. I loved Me-ma, she was the best grandma ever. She was always trying to help out. I needed to make sure to check on her and see how she was holding up since mom's death.

Antonio stepped in the screen door breathing heavy, "I'll go to Granma's house." He'd heard the opportunity as he was walking in and took it. I figured as much, Antonio wouldn't want to be cooped up with our dad for too long. But that was good. He didn't get to know Me-Ma like I did because Anthony raised him separately. Plus, she was getting older and it would be good for them to build some type of relationship.

"Okay, well that's settled," Anthony said suspicious at Antonio's motive for answering so fast, "Andrew, you got the couch, and I will get the air mattress for Jason." I was slightly hurt that my old room had been transformed to a study since Anthony took over mom's house but I didn't want to make an issue of it. I was however curious at all the books Anthony had collected.

"I need to call Mack and let him know I'm in town." I said. Mack was my best friend in Heaven, Texas and now was at the same school with Courtney. Courtney raised her eyebrows and gave me a weird look.

"Why are you looking like that?" I interrogated.

"No reason, it's just that…" She hesitated, "is Mack okay?"

"Well he was feeling ill last time I spoke to him, I need to check on him. Have you seen him since you've been here?"

"Yeah," I replied. Courtney pondered something for a second. "You said he's ill?" I nodded. "Hmm, well you need to let him know to stay in bed. His voice sounds horrible and I think he's a little delirious. He was acting really weird."

"Okay," I said confused, "I'll be sure to pass on the word." She wasn't giving me the full story but I knew if I prodded I couldn't get her to tell me more. Jason jerked up like a deer in headlights out of no where. A sudden look of alarm was in his eyes. I touched his shoulder.

I felt the alarm in my entire being. It was a feeling of being on guard. About what? There was a danger. A strong sense of danger and it was getting close.

I felt something through my abilities. I snapped out of it, "Are you okay, Jason?" I assumed it was something Jason was feeling.

He blinked and tried smiling at me. "Yeah, man, no problem, sorry I thought I forgot something. Can I use your restroom?"

"Sure." I pointed to the door and he went quickly. He wasn't telling me everything and I wished for the life of me that I could get full control of my gift to see what danger he felt. That feeling made me weary.

"Now that Jason is the bathroom, have you boys been okay, you know, spiritually," Anthony asked in a very fatherly tone.

Antonio rolled his eyes and looked at me and then at Anthony. "Yes, Dad, no craziness. Maybe all you had was a bad dream." Anthony had been having dreams about Donyel and Andrea and wasn't sure what to make of it. Since then Antonio had a run in with a demon-man at a club we had gone to at random. Of course Antonio had won. I didn't divulge what I knew because of Antonio's sake. Anthony looked at me for confirmation and I didn't want to lie so I just smiled and shrugged. That wasn't lying right?

"Maybe, Antonio's right." Karen added, "We can't stir up everybody we know because of your dream. Look how mad we made Tamela by questioning her when we got here. Lord knows I don't want any drama with that woman."

"True," Anthony agreed, "Maybe I was wrong. But she was involved with Donyel being conjured the first time and I just had a feeling that maybe...I don't know."

"Are you sure that Donyel is gone," Courtney poked, "that there's no way for him interfering in our lives?"

"Well, if all I had was a dream, then no. I guess." He wasn't sure and I know he didn't feel safe with letting go of his apprehension. Courtney wanted to make sure that Donyel was good and gone for good because he was the reason that her birth father had died. I understood her pain, once again something else we had in common. But the fact remained that I was related to the very monster she hated. Karen wanted to think about something else other than Donyel.

"Anthony, stop worrying so much, Man of God. No weapon formed against you... remember," she said pulling on her strong church up-bringing and faith in God for strength, but I could still sense a tinge of frustration.

"Sorry, this is Christmas time." Anthony forced a smile and attempted to relax. "Let's thank God for this time and family."

"That's right," Karen said taking her daughter under her arm, "family."

"Okay, are we done? Cause, I'm lactose intolerant and this scene is way too cheesy for me," Antonio said.

Karen threw her dish rag at him. "Boy you need to quit." I excused myself from the group and grabbed the phone and went to my old room—now library study. I dialed Mack's number.

"ANDREW, YOU'RE HOME." He answered.

"Whoa, man I didn't even hear the phone

ring." His voice did sound kind of groggy, "Man is your cold getting worse?"

"I'M FEELING BETTER, STILL FIGHTING WITH A LITTLE SOMETHING, BUT I'LL WIN IN THE END." He laughed, giving me the creeps because he really didn't sound like himself.

"Look, uh, so are you gonna come over?"

"THANK YOU FOR THE INVITATION. I WOULD LOVE TO COME OVER. I'LL BE THERE IN AN INSTANT." He hung up. Yep, it sounded as if he needed to lighten up on the cough syrup cause ol' boy was not sounding like himself. Courtney peeked in. Her freshly pressed afro hair dangled long against her shoulders. I was mesmerized by her beauty for a moment.

"Hey are you finished? I want to call Leonard and tell him where I'm staying and my cell phone isn't getting a signal in this town."

I gave the fakest smile I could. "Sure, no problem." I rolled my eyes when she wasn't looked and I thought that maybe I should unplug the base of the portable phone while she was in mid-conversation. But that would be just wrong. I walked back into the living area and Antonio was trying to get some channels on the old TV set that we had in the house. I should've told him that we didn't have cable. Jason was outside standing on the porch. The wind was blowing his jacket to and fro. He was staring out to nothing. I opened the screen door and joined him.

"Hey dude, you okay? You seem kind of dazed, ya know?"

"I'm cool." He smiled back at me, "thanks for your concern." I tried my best to relate with his feeling without getting too scary.

"Jason, sometimes, I.." I chose my words carefully, "I sense that you're upset about something. Is there something that you'd like to talk about?" It was cold. He stood out still looking out to nothing and the cold didn't phase him. I thought that perhaps he didn't even hear me.

"Who's Donyel?" He asked. I think I felt my heart drop. I knew that the thin walls of the house weren't thick enough, "I overheard you guys talking from the bathroom?"

"He's just…" think Andrew think, "an old family member that always causes trouble when he comes around. You know every family has one."

"You're right." Jason nodded, "I have one just like that too."

"Is that why you're upset?" I said looking at him with concern.

He looked at me knowing he couldn't hide too much, "You are so perceptive. Yes, Andrew, that's why. I'm just thinking about my family and hoping that my crazy relative doesn't start any trouble during this time."

"You're real protective over your family

huh?" I asked.

"Yep."

"Me, too I can relate with that. There've been times when I've felt like I was the only one who could do anything to protect my family. That's a lot of pressure to hold."

Jason nodded, "You're right. We're a lot alike, you and me, but just know, Andrew, that you don't have to take on all that pressure by yourself. And you don't have to save your family from every bad thing out there. God has taken care of a lot just remember to surrender a lot of those problems."

"So is that why you're not rushing home? So you can allow God to do his thing?" Andrew asked.

"God is always doing his thing, Andrew." It was the waiting on God to do his thing that I had problem with. Sure, I believed that God was always doing something it's just that it wasn't always obvious to me. The whole saying that all things happen for a reason was becoming so cliché but it was what I put so much of my faith in. It made me feel helpless and I wanted some sort of control of my life and the events that happened. But I guess that was my own issue. I patted his shoulder, Jason had a certain deepness about himself that I could relate to. I liked that. I'm glad that I had like that because with all I was going through I needed someone who could relate at least on some level.

"Well I'm cold, you wanna go back inside," I suggested. My eyes were blinded by a bright light.

Jason squinted, "Someone's driving up."

CHAPTER FOUR

"Hey baby, I'm going to be staying at Andrew's grandmother's house." Courtney said to Leonard on the phone. Her neck was hurting from the way she had the phone lodged between her cheek and her should so she resituated it to the other side.

"I don't like it."

"Like what?" She asked at his strong response, "his grandmother?"

"I don't like that you're spending time around a guy that you apparently used to have a *thing* with." Leonard responded.

"Leo, that's ridiculous, I'm going to be at his grandmother's he's staying at his mother's house."

Leonard gave a long sigh.

"What was that for?" Courtney snapped

back agitated.

"Nothing."

"Look, don't say nothing if it's really something." Courtney was trying to control her volume but she hated when Leonard acted a butt. If there was something bothering him she wanted to know and honestly she didn't see the harm with her staying where she said she was.

"Why are you spending Christmas with them anyhow? Why not with my family, you're my girl!"

"You are always welcome to come here, Leonard."

"You don't get it."

"What am I supposed to be getting!" Courtney realized that her volume had attracted a little attention so she moved herself and the phone into the bathroom. She rested her head against the door and felt like clawing down the side with her nails in all her frustration.

"What if I decided to just hang with my ex-girlfriend over Christmas? How would that make you feel?"

"Well, you know Leonard, I wouldn't feel too bad, you're welcome to go to the hospital as much as you want and visit Tonya if you want to."

"That's not what I mean, it's the principles behind this!" Courtney put the phone on her other ear and stared into the mirror, she could see through her own body language how mad she becoming.

"The only principle is, that you don't trust me."

"I trust you but it just aint right."

"So what do you want? You want me to diss a long time friend of the family…no his whole family and friends because you don't like him?"

"Yes."

Courtney didn't want to talk anymore in fear that she would really have to tell Leonard off, but she knew how he was and he would continue to argue until he won. She didn't understand why he had to be so stubborn in his views. "Look, I'm going to talk to you later." She said, "You're talking out of your mind, Merry Christmas."

"Oh, so *now* you believe in Christmas."

"Shut up." She hung up the phone. The knock at the door startled her.

"I'll be right out."

"You okay?" It was Antonio. "You sounded kinda mad there." Courtney cracked open the door and tried to regain her composure by slowly breathing out.

"When did you start eavesdropping Tonio?"

"You made it sorta easy to do. Who was that, Leonard?" Courtney always had this undeniable connection with Antonio since the first time they met. Antonio just had a way with the opposite sex even if they were just friends. In a nutshell, when Antonio opened the doors of communication, women talked and they enjoyed it and Courtney would be no exception.

"Yep." She sighed and looked up and off.

"Hey, unfold those arms and quit looking like the grinch." Antonio said trying to make her laugh. She cracked a smile and let her arms down.

"I don't know what's up with you men and why you have to war with each other so much. And then what's worse he has the nerve to tell me what to do."

"Wait," he said pausing her obvious venting, "what's he bossing you about?"

"He doesn't want me hanging around you guys."

"Want me to beat em up for ya?" Antonio

punched his fists into his hand.

Courtney giggled, "No, he's my boyfriend, Antonio."

"Gee, sorry."

"Funny. It's just that all this started because of a girl. And now, Leonard and Andrew still can't be cool because of me."

"Ah, Leonard's a butthead, from what Andrew's been telling me, the guy has always picked on him. The question is how is that the good girls always go for the thugs?"

Courtney tilted her head, "So now *you're* on me?"

"Courtney, Leonard is obviously not right for you. Ya'll are so completely different."

"So I should be with who? Andrew? Because we're so much alike?"

"Hey," Antonio raised his nonverbal white flag, "I didn't suggest Andrew. He has his own things he is trying to deal with. I know ya'll had your thing and that he is still into you, but love is a two way street. There's no point in him loving you if you don't love him." He paused, she stood there thinking for a moment, "You don't love him right?"

Courtney looked puzzled by the question, "Love him? I love Andrew…as a person." She stuttered over her words.

"That's not what I mean." Antonio was about to explain but Courtney eyes shut closed and she jerked real quick as if she just got shocked by something.

"Whoa, I just felt like I had a déjà vu" Courtney said.

"You mean right now?"

"Wait.." She looked around as if she was trying to figure something out, "I've seen all this before."

"What?" Antonio asked.

"Shhh," She demanded, afraid that his

talking would interfere. She looked around and into the bathroom mirror. She saw a quick vision of Mack jumping at her. She squealed and grabbed Antonio's arm.

"What?"

"I saw a vision of …I don't know. There's something not right. Where's Andrew?" Antonio looked at the sudden fright in here eyes. He took her outside.

CHAPTER FIVE

Donyel in one thought brought Tamela and the cat-incarnated Philip onto the neighborhood street not far from the house. It took Tamela some time to bring herself to realization to where they were. Donyel turned and glanced and gave her a small smile sensing her thoughts.

"What are we here for?" She asked.

"It's all a part of my plan, sweet Tamela." Donyel said turning back in the direction to where he wanted to go.

"What about Tonya? Are you going to bring her back?" She said grabbing on his arm. His skin was hard and cold as stone. Like a magnet being repelled from another like pole she was pushed back by an unseen force.

"Don't..." Donyel said calmly, "touch me." Tamela humbly pulled herself off the ground and Philip hesitantly scooted up next to her. "Now if you must know, my plan is simple. This family has done their best effort to get in my way and now I will get in theirs."

"But Lord Donyel," Tamela dusted herself off and held her arm, "what is going to keep them from doing to you what they did before? They know things that can bind you and if I lose you then I lose..."

"You will not lose your daughter, have faith. But my ultimate plan still remains the same. A new age is approaching and soon I will be able to align myself as ruler. I need an agent to do my bidding and be my blood here on earth; One that will rid of all those who are against me and to whom I can bestow my power. I will be the father and he will be the son. He will be the nemesis to all who oppose me and strengthen my blood line once more so I can reign as king."

"But father, I will do as you will if you would only grant me a suitable body and power again." Philip said licking Donyel toes.

Donyel kicked the poor cat into the bushes, "Not you, you imbecile, I'm speaking of the twins."

"Andrew and Antonio, both of them?" Tamela asked.

"No, I will only need one, the strongest of the two."

Tamela shook her head, "I don't mean to be disrespectful, my Lord, but these are Anthony Turner's son's and he's very much human." Donyel's face cringed slightly when she said this. He knew this truth but didn't want that to put doubt in his mind, "If they are anything like him, and I assume they are, I doubt if they will see things your way. Look what they did to my daughter. But the fact remains, they have my

DNA in their blood."

"They are only human. And everybody, every family has a weakness. I will find that weakness and break the bonds of kinship to Anthony Turner's son….and he will become my son. Philip!" Donyel called into the bushes and the cat fearfully came out into the open, "return to the house, stay with the woman, Karen. I will follow the boys."

Tamela begged Donyel, "But when they see you…"

"That's just it…they won't see me." Like a chameleon, Donyel faded into the shadows, his eyes the only slightly visible and then there was nothing but the whispery wind of his voice. Tamela looked around for him and felt all around to no avail . She wrapped her arms around her breasts and she felt chills crawl almost all through her.

"Donyel?"

"Shhh." She felt his voice breeze around her. "Go to your daughter, and wait for my instructions. I will take over from here." With his powers he transported Tamela back into the woods in a whirlwind. When she opened her eyes she was over where she had parked car .

She looked around. No Donyel, no little scary cat; she rummaged in her purse for her keys and jumped in her car. Could she have seen what she thought she had seen? She held onto the car steering wheel with both hands and took an exhale. She was nervous to what she had unleashed. Donyel was mad, she knew it, but Tamela didn't care. She wanted Tonya back and he was the only one who could do that for her.

She started her car and drove back into town and to the hospital. She was sure to grab some flowers from the local florist before she got there. She smiled at the nurse at the front desk who didn't say anything to her. They had become so familiar with seeing her come in every day that it had become second nature. Tamela normally hated hospitals, the smell, the feeling she got when she walked in as if death himself walked the halls waiting to see if the harvest was ripe. She didn't want her daughter to be in that harvest.

She stood in the doorway looking into dim lit room. The beeping sound of the heart monitor was the only thing that could be heard. Tonya, laid on the bed, staring into nothing. Medically the doctors said she was a vegetable. Tamela went over to the side of the bed of her daughter.

"Hey baby, I brought you some flowers." She placed the flowers in the vase. "Oh you're so beautiful, here let me put some light in here." She flicked on the lamp next to bed. "There, that's better."

She pulled a brush out her purse and

lifted Tonya's head and situated herself behind Tonya so that she could brush her hair. "So pretty, my pretty girl. Your grandpa, Donyel, will make you better. So pretty, child of the angels." She started to cry and wiped her tears. Tonya was all she had in the world, Tonya was her very soul, and to lose her daughter was to lose herself.

"Come back to me, pretty baby, don't…" She kissed the crown of her head, "don't leave me alone." She wished that Tonya had never got involved with the Turners but she knew it was all in Donyel's will.

"Ma'am." The nurse said peeking in the door, "I'm sorry but visiting hours will be over in ten minutes."

"It's okay, I'm done." She kissed Tonya.

CHAPTER SIX

"Andrew, my boy!" Mack said getting out his car. Jason grabbed my shoulder and I looked back at him. He looked tense. He let go and I tried not to think about Jason's reaction.

"Hey Mack, glad to see you're feeling better," I waved to him.

"Yes, I'm feeling great." I gave him a hug. Chills. *I saw a vision of Mack in the bathroom struggling and screaming and pulling at the handles on the door, his hands straining and pulling at what he could. Something was holding onto him, restraining him, almost absorbing him?*

I jerked back. "Mack are you okay?"

He gave me a crafty smile. "I said I'm feeling great. Is your brother here as well?"

I couldn't understand why he was asking me this. "Yeah, Antonio is in there. Why?"

"JUST WONDERING. I GUESS YOU GUYS HAVE COME TOGETHER FOR DONYEL." My heart jumped and I looked at Jason and then at Mack.

"Uh, not really, Donyel's not here."

Mack closed his eyes and shifted his head to the left and right as if he was sensing something. "OH, BUT HE IS."

I pulled Mack to the side beyond Jason's hearing.

"What are you doing? Do you want Jason to find out everything? Why are you talking about Donyel?"

"WHY AREN'T *YOU* TELLING ME ABOUT DONYEL?"

"Donyel's gone!" I told him, "That's just my dad being paranoid." Mack looked as if he was getting upset and squared up in my face.

"LOOK, ANDREW, I HAVE SOME THINGS I

NEED TO SETTLE WITH DONYEL AND YOU WILL NOT GET IN MY WAY. I CAN FEEL HIS PRESENCE EVERYWHERE NOW." He pushed me and I fell to the ground. "WHERE IS HE!"

"Mack what's wrong with you!" I yelled, amazed at his strength.

Jason ran up. "Aye!" Mack clutched Jason by the shirt as he ran up and slung him to the ground with no effort.

Courtney ran through the door. "Andrew!" Her distraction was too much and Mack grabbed me once again and lifted me into the air by the collar, "LAST TIME, WHERE IS DONYEL!"

"I don't know what you're talking about!" Antonio came through the door and ran toward Mack who had me practically dangling in the air. It was horrible déjà vu from a few years back and I was trying to understand where Mack had gotten all this strength. When Antonio reached Mack, Mack simply turned his head and gave a look. Antonio slammed directly into a protective shield that surrounded us.

"Andrew!" Antonio said on the ground rubbing his head, "turn your shield off."

"It's not me! I didn't do it. He's got my protective power some how." I struggled to break free of his grip. Dad and Karen were now outside.

"Boys!" Dad yelled.

"Courtney, what's going on?" Karen yelled.

"Mack, let him go!" Courtney pleaded. I knew that whatever was going on, after all that I had experienced in my life, and what I had seen in my vision, this wasn't Mack, Mack had been possessed by some being. Whatever it was, it knew Donyel.

"Who are you?" I grunted and choked in his hold.

"JUST AN OLD FRIEND OF THE FAMILY YOU CAN SAY. AND ANDREW YOU'RE HOLDING OUT ON ME." His grip on my shirt and my neck was tight even though he showed little effort. I thought about how Tonya lost her mind when she got possessed and I was hoping that Mack wouldn't end up the same way. But how? Mack wasn't a witch. How did this thing take over him and get to us?

"What have you done with Mack?"

"MACK IS HERE, WITH ME." The pupil of his eyes were large and black and hollow in their look, "YOU CARE SO MUCH FOR HIM." He let me go with a push and I fell to the ground next to Antonio.

"I KNOW YOU'RE HERE DONYEL! AND I WILL GET MY REVENGE!" He yelled in the air and spinned around snarling in anger as if he could sense something everybody else couldn't.

"Use your new power," I whispered to

Antonio.

"I really don't know how to make it start," he whispered back. Mack grunted and tumbled over holding his stomach.

"Andrew…" I heard the weak familiar voice of my friend. He was on his knees and his whole face was red. Tears were coming from his eyes and his forehead was straining as if he was in agonizing pain. He reached for me. "Andrew…help me. It's in me." I reached for him but Antonio pulled me back.

"It could be a trick." I pushed him away and crawled over to my friend.

"Dude, what's in you? What is it?"

Mack tumbled over and let his head hit my shoulder. "The ring," he whispered. I looked at the ring that he said he found and it was tightly fit to his finger. I tried to pull it off but once again Mack switched on me.

"GET BACK!" Mack pushed my chest and

I rolled like a tumble weed.

"Andrew!" Dad yelled but Karen held him back realizing that we were at the mercy of something unknown. Antonio's rage grew even more and charged forward hitting Mack low before he knew what happened. We were engulfed in a flash of light.

Antonio had done it. He managed to jump between time but this time he pulled both me and Mack into the dimension. He was wrestling with the spirited Mack on the ground and when he grazed by me that's when I was pulled in with them. When I gathered my wits, I noticed it wasn't Mack Antonio was wrestling with. It was something else. Another angel? The angelic being was youthful, and tall with a head full of wild hair. Antonio continued to handle the situation swinging the being into the air. Antonio was far stronger in this realm. Even I, myself, felt this surge of power.

"Andrew!" I heard a voice. Mack was over on the ground, wrapped in ethereal chains. I ran over to him but he was snatched up in the air by the flying being.

"Close, but he belongs to me!" He laughed. That made me mad. I jumped and seemed to fly up to him with no effort. Before he noticed I grabbed Mack.

"Andrew!" Antonio yelled. Mack looked scared but I held on to Mack's legs while the spirit-thing flew holding on to the chains that bound Mack.

"Let him go!" I demanded.

"Okay," He said and I regretted my last request suddenly. He let go and I plummeted toward the ground holding onto Mack.

"Andrew!!!" Antonio screamed. I closed my eyes and prepared for the inevitable but before I knew it I elevated back into the air.

"You're flying!" Mack said.

"I guess so."

"So where are your wings?" he tried to joke.

"Not the time, Mack, not the time." From the sky I could see Antonio looking up and deep in the shadows behind him...

"Donyel."

"what?" Mack said. He faded back into the shadows. I knew what I saw. I levitated down to the ground.

"Where'd you get the ability to do that?" Antonio said.

"Well I can't, I don't think." I scratched my head, "I think being in this realm makes us a little bit stronger." Mack struggled to get free.

"Well in that case," Antonio pulled at the chains and they broke like tissue paper.

"Thanks." Mack said. The spirit floated to the ground.

"Do you think I would make it that easy?

This isn't the physical the world, you are in the spiritual. He is still mine." He raised his hand, there was a ring attached and the jewel glowed. Mack disappeared from in between us and his spirit was sucked into the ring.

"Give him back!" I threatened. Antonio held me back.

"I will when I get what I want."

"Donyel." I sighed. I wasn't sure what he wanted us to do.

"Donyel is gone. He's been bound for years." Antonio yelled back.

"You're all fools, and I will destroy you all one by one." He began to walk away.

"Wait!" I ran forward. He stopped. "Who are you, why do you want Donyel?"

"You're the empath, son of Heaven, you should know who I am." I looked at him. He reached his hand out inviting me to know. I slowly walked up.

"Andrew no." Antonio yelled from behind. I didn't listen I touched his fingertips. In that moment I saw it all. The throne, the King, Donyel, the battle, the curse of the ring, and the countless number of people that had fallen under its wrath. Thousands of men had come into possession of the ring and it had brought the wealth and fortune and in return they lost their souls.

I let go, *"Ibo, the jinn."* I said and he nodded.

"What the hell is a jinn?" Antonio commented. I shook my head and looked at Antonio to be patient.

"So you're doing all this to get back at Donyel? You've waited all these years?"

"But now, I've found a connection. You two." He pointed at me and Antonio.

"Look, we're not on his side."

"But you are his offspring. You're

protecting him."

"We aint on his side, man!" Antonio yelled back.

"Tonio, chill." I reprimanded him, "I got this."

"I don't like how you talking to me Drew."

Ibo grew impatient, "I don't have time for this sibling rivalry."

"No wait, look, please let my friend go, and I will find Donyel for you. I will help you. We have the power to stop Donyel."

"We?" Antonio stated. I ignored him.

"So what do you propose Son of Heaven?"

"Let Mack go, and I will help you get Donyel." Ibo walked around me and smiled. He was thinking deeply.

"I don't like this Andrew."

"Chill, Antonio." I took a breath of

desperation.

"You agree to help me?" Ibo asked once more.

"Yes.".

"Excellent, and when you accomplish your goal, I will release your friend."

"Agreed." I answered and held my hand out.

"Then we have a..." He grabbed my hand, "deal!" A surge of energy blasted when he grabbed my hand and I felt like I was being electrocuted.

"Andrew no!" Antonio advanced toward me but blasts of energy kept him from getting close. Ibo fade away and I fell to my knees.

Antonio ran to my side, "You okay?"

I nodded my head, "I'm fine."

"Oh no." He said.

"What?" I asked back looking at my brother's frustrated look. On my hand, tightly

fit…was the ring.

CHAPTER SEVEN

In a blink everything was back to normal. I look around and Mack was lying on the ground passed out. Antonio was on the ground as well.

Courtney ran over, "Are you guys okay? There was a flash of light when Antonio knocked into Mack and you guys were passed out." I shook it off and picked myself up.

"How long were we out?" I asked. Antonio picked himself off the ground rubbing his head.

"about a minute." She replied looking worried. Dad and Karen ran over to make sure everything was okay.

"What just happened here? Andrew? Antonio? What's going on?" Dad said giving us a stern look. I looked at my hand and the ring was still on my hand. I looked at Antonio's expression and I could tell that he remembered the whole battle too. Mack still lay there on the ground passed out. I began to worry.

"Dad we need to get Mack to a hospital, something is really wrong with him." Karen ran back inside to call 911.

"Boys…what's going on?"

"Dad, I don't want you to worry okay." I told him.

"It's Donyel." He sighed and had this frustrated look, "How is he doing this!" He yelled and walked back to the porch and flopped down on the steps wringing his hands over and over.

Antonio looked at me, "the ring, it's on your hand."

"I know," I whispered back to him.

"Are you okay, I mean—is Ibo,"

"I don't feel different, but I can feel like

there's something around me, maybe he can't take over me cause he's trying to keep Mack at the same time."

"Or you're too powerful."

Courtney butted in, "what are you guys talking about? Ibo, who's that?" I looked over at her and gave her shush so that dad wouldn't get involved.

"It's a long story Courtney, and maybe this is a good time for you not to get too much into this."

"Something just happened here, and it's got Mack, and you don't want me to be involved?"

I got a little heated, "You were the one who said you wanted a normal life"

"Hey, not now." Antonio interrupted, "Courtney, this is really dangerous, Andrew doesn't want you to get hurt. It involves Donyel and this other guy and we're stuck in the middle of it now." Jason picked himself off the ground and came to. Antonio went over to tend to him to make sure he was all right.

"Man what happened?" Jason grunted, "I feel like I was hit by a bus."

"Something like that," Antonio told him, "here, let's go in the house." He said escorted him back inside.

Courtney wanted answers."Why are you stuck? Just walk away." Courtney said.

"We have to help Mack," I knelt beside my friend and held his head in my lap, he was breathing hard as if he were warring with something, "This is spiritual, some kind of …angel called a jinn has control over him."

"A jinn?" Courtney slapped her forehead, "Another angel?"

"Yeah, can you go online and see how much information you can find out about these things?"

"Wait, what are you..."

"Please, Courtney, we need as much information as possible, and next to Dad you're our best demon guru." I pleaded with her. She held her peace and nodded.

"Okay, I'll see what I can find." The local ambulance was there in no time and picked up Mack, I watched as the paramedics took him away on the stretcher. Antonio came back outside and I could sense that he knew I was upset about the whole situation. Antonio patted my shoulder, "We'll help him don't worry."

"I just don't want what happened to Tonya..."

"Hey," he stopped me, "we're gonna save him, don't worry about it."

Dad called us back in the house for a family meeting. Everyone sat in the den including Jason and I wasn't sure how I was going to explain what had happened but I felt that he needed to be informed just in case.

All the fellas sat on the couch, Karen sat on the armchair, Courtney sat cross-legged on the floor.

Dad paced the floor, "Boys," he said probing like the bad cop, "I want some answers. What happened out there?"

"I don't know what to tell you." Antonio shrugged dismissing the question.

"Guys, this is not the time, if Donyel is up to something we all need to do something." Karen insisted.

"Perhaps you should tell your Dad, Andrew." Courtney added.

Wow, how did this all turn back to me I wondered. I rubbed the ring on my hand with my thumb and looked around the room, "I'm not quite sure myself Dad. Donyel may have something to do with what happened and if he does then I'm going to stop him."

"You're going to stop him? No sir, you're not!"

"Andrew means we're going to stop him." Antonio jumped on my side.

Dad looked at both of us crazy, "Do you realize what we're dealing with here? Donyel is not some demon or something that can be stopped easily. This is an angel for God's sake!"

"An angel?" Jason asked. I knew this was going to be hard for him but he was being plunged into this head first.

"I'm sorry we have to break this to you like this but this is real serious and if Donyel's back then you need to know what's going on Jason." I told him.

"Who's Donyel?"

"Remember all we used to learn in Bible study about spirits and principalities Jason?" I asked him. He nodded.

"Well," I chose my words carefully,

"there's angels and then there are fallen angels."

"Like Lucifer." He seemed to be catching on.

"Yeah, exactly and well Donyel is a fallen angel that's been tormenting our family for quite some time."

He looked at me and then at Antonio, "You're serious."

"Yeah. If this is too much I mean, we can take you home, but this is real dangerous."

"Too dangerous," Dad interrupted me, "for you and your brother to think that you're going after him."

"What do you expect us to do Dad? Just sit here and wait for him to come after us?" Antonio's tone was snapping.

"No, but we do need a plan of action and will not have you boys going out there getting hurt."

"We can handle it. We have powers for a reason." Antonio said.

"Whoa, powers?" Jason asked.

"Um, I'll explain the rest of that later." I told him, "Look, Dad we can't really afford to wait. Mack's been hurt and we need..."

"--and I don't want you guys getting hurt as well! Don't you understand..."

"You're the one who doesn't understand Dad! We're not kids anymore," Antonio argued.

"You're *my* kids!"

"Anthony! please stop yelling," Karen intervened. I didn't want to tell Dad about Ibo. I felt that Donyel was enough stress. I knew in my mind that I was going to keep to the plan of action that I already had set. I needed to help Mack at whatever cost and I was running out of time. I wasn't going to let him be a vegetable. I couldn't bear that type of guilt. I said whatever I needed to appease my father.

"What do you want us to do, Dad?" He took a breath and rubbed his temple. He looked as if he was going to blow a gasket.

"What I want is for you to do nothing…at least for right now. And don't go using your powers. *No* powers." He looked at Antonio.

"Whatever," Antonio mumbled, "you act like we're the bad guys or something."

"No it's not that. But you know Donyel wants you. You just make it easier for him to find you when you do that."

"Dad, I think he knows where we are, we don't know where *he* is." There was a scratch at the door.

"Well, I don't think we're going to let Donyel or any other devil keep us from living," Karen said going to the door, "I think what your dad wants us to do is depend on God for answers and that's what we're going to do." She said trying to ease the situation. She opened the door.

"Loopy! There you are !" The cat pranced inside rubbing itself on the furniture and moving into the den with the rest of the family. "Well at least some good came out of today."

"Let's get some rest," Dad said, "We'll all get back together tomorrow and be on your guard, pray and if you see or feel anything peculiar get a hold of one of us." The meeting dismissed itself and Dad and Karen retreated to his room, obviously he was upset and she felt the need to console him. I went and grabbed the book, Heaven Sent.

"Jason, I think you should read this."
"What is this?"
"It's a book I wrote."
"Man, I didn't know your wrote a book! This isn't your name on the front though."
"No, that way I can keep somewhat of a private life," I told him and took hold of the book.

He looked at me curiously. "This book is about you?"

"Yeah, it's about what's happened in the past few years. I would have a hard time explaining everything but I think my memoirs will help you."

"Yeah, watch out though. He starts putting your private stuff in the book once you become his friend," Antonio warned. I glared back.

Courtney picked up her bags preparing to leave, "I noticed you didn't tell you Dad about Ibo."

"Very observant, we're still sticking to our plan, I just didn't want to get Dad too upset." I again gave Antonio a look.

"What? Why you looking at me? I just can't stand how he's always trying to control what we do and how he's just—ya know, holding us back."

"He's not holding us…"

"You don't get it, Andrew, when I was in school I could play any and all sports because of my strength. Dad was always like, 'Antonio you need to pull back, Antonio don't win every race, Antonio don't play perfect *all* the time or somebody will notice and question what's going on.' I hated that I couldn't be myself!"

"I'm sure he was just trying to protect you," Courtney said.

"It's just that if I have the ability to do something, I should do it. It's not my fault that I can do supernatural things, I was born with a gift and it's not fair that I have to suppress myself because Dad thinks it's evil."

"He's a different generation and he's basing his opinions on what he's been through. You're not going to change Dad by arguing with him."

"Andrew's right," Courtney cosigned me,

"I'm gonna do some researching, luckily I have my laptop with me. I'll have some info for you guys tomorrow."

"Cool, Let's try and get some rest despite of what happened. We're going to need it."

Everyone agreed and Antonio and Courtney left to Me-ma's house.

CHAPTER EIGHT

The smell of warm cookies on the oven filled Me-Ma's house. The fire in the fireplace crackled and flickered dimly, lighting the room. Antonio almost forgot all that had transgressed as he looked inside. The front room appeared to have been modeled from a picture from *Country Home and Gardens Magazine*. Antonio stood on the porch with his duffle bag in one hand. The door was open but the screen door was closed and he wondered what type of woman was this that had such little regard for security. But this was the country; so different from the crime-infested city life he was so used to.

He peaked through the screen because he didn't want to bust on in the house and startle the woman. Perhaps Me-Ma had a gun; this *was* the country. Karen was still behind at the car getting her bags so Antonio thought that maybe he should wait for her.

When Karen caught up he slowly opened the door and ducked a little to walk through so he wouldn't hit his head.

"Come on in!" The voice was seasoned with a country twain. He hesitated for a second and realized the command was directed at him. Antonio stood at the door but Me-Ma pulled him in with open arms. She held a plate in one hand and insisted he take a bite of one her cinnamon gingersnaps before he take a step further in the house.

Karen had last seen Me-Ma years ago when Antonio was just a baby so she was quite excited to see her again.

Antonio attempted to introduce himself, "Uhh, hey, I'm …"

"Boy I know who you are! Now come on

ova hea' so I can get a good look atcha'!" She sat the plate down on a nearby coffee table and grabbed Antonio's cheeks. Her eyes were filled with unconditional love and she pulled him closer into a hug. Never in his life had he felt so helpless and with all his strength he didn't think he could pull from the hug she gave him—yet it was comforting.

"Wooowee! My! Child you have grown! Lookin' just like Andrew but *I* can see the difference. Mmmhm. Yo daddy used to send me pictures of ya growing up but it's good to finally have you come on and visit yo' granmama."

"Dad sent you pictures of me?" Antonio was shocked by this tidbit of information and lo and behold the woman had what looked like a shrine to her only two grandchildren. Antonio saw a progression in his age from the lower level up to some of his most recent pictures from high school on a shelf. He chuckled to himself. He wasn't sure why but perhaps it was because he never felt so welcome in a strange place. Even though Me-ma was new family to him, he wasn't new to her, she loved him all along.

"Me-ma it's so good to see you again." Karen came in her jovial usual self and grabbed Me-ma in a warming hug. "How's everything been?"

"Oh baby, fine fine…I'm just trying to harvest my greens out back before it get too chilly."

"Mmm, I love some greens Me-ma. I know you gonna cook me some before I leave." Karen smiled in her tone.

Me-ma laughed it off playful slapping her on her arm and grabbed her bag. "You can have Andrea ol' room and Antonio you can have the guest room. Baby, show him where the guest room is," She requested to Karen.

"Yes, ma'am." Karen replied

respectfully. Antonio was still in shock watching this old woman move about with such virility. He followed Karen down the hall. His footsteps echoed loudly on the hollow wooden floor. He ducked through yet another door to the guestroom and plopped down on the spring mattress in the center of the room. It squeaked and creaked under his weight.

"You okay?" Karen looked concerned in the doorway.

Antonio examined his surroundings. "I'm good."

"I mean from what happened tonight, that's what I mean."

Antonio rubbed his head. "Mack's going to be okay…"

"Mack's not whom I'm referring to, Antonio. I'm thinking about what happened with you and your dad. That argument; what was that about?"

Antonio sighed not really wanting to open up that can of worms again but Karen wasn't the one to give up to easily. She rested on the doorpost and leaned her head a little further in to get his eye contact.

"Karen, my dad is just one big control freak. He just always has to be in control of everything. When I was a kid and I wanted to play sports, my powers started showing. I started realizing that I was strong for my size. When he figured that, he freaked." Karen sat down next to him and rubbed his shoulder.

"Karen, he made me feel as if something was wrong with me, as if I was a bad person for the power that I had."

"Your dad doesn't think that. He's just trying to protect you, Antonio."

Antonio curled his lip in skepticism. "Is that why he prayed God bind my powers in the name of Jesus?" Antonio shook his head, "He told me that I should pray more, that I wasn't close enough to God. Then he forbade me for trying out anymore for sports—said that I was cheating. How is it cheating if I'm doing what I'm capable of doing? But I tried out anyways, despite what he said."

"Well, if you're supernaturally strong it's not…"

"…Fair. I know. You want to know what I think is not fair? I think it's not fair that I never got to have a relationship with my mother. I think it's not fair that my own father treats me like I'm some kind of monster. I think it's not fair that I don't know who or what I am and no one could really tell me! I figured that for the type of life I've been dealt I deserve a little joy just once. Balance things out, that's fair to me." Antonio stopped to repress his emotions. He wasn't sure why tonight he was venting and that alone was upsetting.

He wrote it off quickly in his mind. "I don't wanna talk about this anymore." He got up from the bed.

"Hey Antonio," Karen said with the most concerned look on her face.

He looked back with a blank stare masking his true emotions.

"Andrea's gone I know. I'm sorry, she'll be missed and no one can bring her back. But…" Karen reached out without moving at all, "If you need someone, don't be afraid to talk to me." It meant so much more. It meant more to Antonio even though he cared not to show it.

He looked away so she couldn't see his eyes water. "Aiight, I 'preciate it." He moved past her to leave the room.

The house was lined with pictures of unfamiliar smiling faces on the wall. One of which he almost recognized as his own mother. He paused a moment to see her picture. The picture had a reddish haze to its color, common with older photographs. The girl in the picture smiled like she didn't have a care in the world. He kept walking not to let his emotions get taken too far down the hall way of memories.

He went a little further to next door on the right which was an empty room that looked like it should be for a kid. It had a pink canopy bed with frill and dolls on it. A girl's room—the only girl it could have belonged to was his mother. In the corner was an old deflated basketball and soccer ball telling him that his mother was anything but the average girly girl. He sat on the squeaky bed. Antonio peeked in the drawer of the nightstand next to bed to find a small book with child-like writing inside.

"Another journal, maybe Andrew would like to read this to create another book." He put it back in and decided to rejoin the group in the living room. Karen and Courtney had already made themselves comfortable and were sipping peppermint tea to go along with their gingersnaps. Me-Ma definitely had the southern hospitality down to a T. Antonio spied Me-Ma's cat rubbing his back on the floor belly up and staring back at Antonio upside down. He was a fat lil sucker Antonio thought and figured this guy had not missed a meal. Almost as if the cat read Antonio's mind, the cat walked off insulted with a bow-legged waddle.

"You want some tea, Baby?" Me-Ma asked Antonio. He shook his head feeling slightly awkward at how the woman looked as if she knew him so well and he didn't know that much about her. But he sucked it up because that's why he had decided to come here in the first place.

"Momma Wallace, it's been so long," Karen said getting her attention, "I love how you've decorated the house." There were all types of Christmas holly and tinsel adorning the shelves and walls.

"Aw, thank ya, Baby," Me-Ma said to Karen pouring her some more tea, "Ya'll make ya' self at home now, if you get too cold there's some logs for the fire by the side of the house and I got some extra blankets in the closet. I'm gon' get me some rest now," She said shuffling off into the back to her room.

"She's so sweet." Admired Karen.

"Why you looking like a lost little boy Antonio?" Courtney observed.

"Huh?" Antonio said trying to snap out of his zoning trance. He couldn't help it. The house was cornucopia of sensory overload. The smell of the tea and cookies, the sound of the crackling fire, the sight of the holiday lights blinking in the window…he was convinced, his grandmother was Mrs. Claus.

"I think I'm going to get ready for bed

too. I have to get up early and get Christmas dinner ready." Karen said and made her way to the room. Courtney watched as her mother left the room and quickly shuffled into her backpack and got out her laptop.

"Come on …come on, give me a connection," She petitioned the computer.

"What are you doing?" Antonio said, all this Christmas stuff and made him forget the present mission.

"I found a couple of sites about the Jinn and saved them to my favorites. Look at this." She pointed at the screen and there was a website breaking down different types of spirits, angels, and demons. The jinn was one class, come to the world in a fallen state just like the fallen angels. If anything, as Antonio and Courtney read it sounded…

"This sounds almost exactly like the story of the fallen angels and the Nephilim." Antonio said.

"Except most of the Jinn stories come from Islamic mythology and not Jewish or Christian" Courtney explained scrolling through the page, "This is where we get the mythology of Genies, another variation of the world Jinn. Turns out, there's a myth that King Solomon controlled the jinn with a ring and made them build his temple for him. Any jinn that didn't bow in reverence to God, he bound up in jars sealed with the ring."

Antonio laughed, "Solomon put the genies in magic lamps? Get outta here!"

Courtney kept a serious face, "It's a only a myth, but a lot of myth is based on truth or oral history and becomes myth after years of getting passed down."

"But nobody has rubbed any lamps or opened any crazy jars so... wait." Antonio thought about what she had just said. "The ring, he had a ring. Andrew has a ring now that Mack had before he went berserk. Is there anything in there about a Jinn named Ibo?"

"No, I mean, there's stories about all types of spirits that Solomon dealt with but it doesn't give names. Do you think that the ring Andrew has is actually…"

"I don't know," Antonio interrupted, "But crazier things have happened. If it is, Andrew has a powerful ring on his hand that's capable of doing a whole lot of things. Evidently Ibo is connected to it some how."

"That's pretty scary, for something that ancient to be on Andrew. How's he handling it?" Courtney asked with concern.

Antonio sat on the couch next to her. "Okay, I guess, but after seeing what it allowed Ibo to do to Mack I'm a little worried. Andrew is not that strong."

Courtney closed her laptop. "No, not

physically. But don't underestimate the strength of your brother's heart."

CHAPTER NINE

I woke up gasping for my breath. I had a nightmare or least what I thought may had been one. Ibo was in it and I was in a funhouse full of mirrors. I couldn't tell if he was chasing me or if I was chasing him but all I could see was his reflection zipping through the maze. What scared me the most was looking into my reflection and seeing his image laughing. Perhaps I was in over my head, I was still learning all this spiritual stuff but here I was in something I knew completely nothing about. Maybe Dad was right to want to protect me from knowing all this. But living in fear was something I couldn't do. These were the cards I had been dealt in life and I had been given a gift (even though it felt like a curse sometimes).

I quietly got up from the couch and went to the bathroom. I needed to wash the beads of sweat that were on my face. I didn't want to make a lot of noise so I tip-toed and searched for the light switch. I closed the door gently and flicked on the light. I turned the water on softly so it made no more than a soft whistle in the quiet of the night and sprinkled my face with my fingers. Then there was a noise.

I stood still, not wanting to make a sound. Must be Jason, but then I heard a whisper, not my dad but someone talking with Jason. Then I noticed something else. The light whistle of the water from the faucet had stopped—but I hadn't turned the water off. I looked down in the sink, the water was frozen. Not like ice, but suspended. Stopping or transcending time wasn't my power as well, was it? I listened to the door, evidently someone else hadn't been affected. I turned the light off hoping who ever out there wouldn't notice and cracked open the door enough so that I could see.

Jason was standing in the living room talking to what looked like, from what I remember, an angel. A big one, He was really tall, with long white hair and draped in a long red toga-like robe, his skin was about as white as his hair. Some unknown breeze kept him hovering over Jason but he didn't seem disturbed by it's presence.

"You're manifesting, why?" The angel asked Jason.

"I am following orders. Someone needs to be here who can transition them better into their calling."

"There are others destined to do that for you."

"But until then...I'm here, they've already been attacked a couple of times. But I'm sure you have much to do yourself. This household is definitely in need of the holiday spirit."

"I sense that, that is my purpose."

"Good luck, they're not an easy family to…"

I left my hiding place and interrupted the meeting. "No, we're very complicated." They both looked my direction in shock.

Jason looked at the angel. "I thought you stopped time."

The angel, bewildered, whispered back, "I did." I just shook my head and smiled at both of them, "You should know by now that I'm not very typical and usually the laws of the universe are bent when it comes to me, but you Jason— who are you really, and who is this guy?" I asked pointing at what looked like a very young model version of Chris Kringle.

"Um, Andrew…you're tired. It's just a dream," Jason said.

"Dream my foot!" But before I could

argue any further Jason touched my mouth with his hand. "Shhhh," He said staring into my eyes. His hypnotic stare made my head light and I felt my knees slowly buckle. Next thing I knew, all was dark.

I woke up gasping for air, back on the couch.

I peeked over in the darkness at Jason who still up reading with a small light pen. "You okay?" he asked. "I heard you groaning in your sleep, I didn't want to bother you just in case you were having a girly dream."

"Funny," I whispered. Maybe it was dream after all. "Nah, I was having a nightmare. I guess too much is on my mind."

"Well, you got a lot on my mind, I haven't been able to put your book down but I know I need to rest." Jason took a second glance at me and reiterated, " Are you sure you're okay?" I was sweating so I guess he had just cause. I nodded and wiped the sweat from my brow. The room was dimly lit by the blinking Christmas lights Karen had adorned the room with. Jason put the book away and looked up toward the ceiling.

"You ever get scared of what's out there, Andrew?"

"Sometimes," I contemplated, "It's like, I've heard about angels my whole life in church, in movies, but you just never really know what's really going on in this world. To me it's like we're living this life but in actuality there's a whole other world co-existing along side ours that most people have no idea about."

"So would you freak out if you met a real angel?"

"I met one. His name was Shariel," I told Jason, "He didn't hang around long though and I haven't seen him since, well, the last time Donyel tried interfering in our lives. I think he's like my guardian angel or something."

"That's pretty cool. I believe in angels and I don't think you have anything to worry about. If the good angels are on your side you'll be okay."

"Yeah I guess so, it's just that…" I paused as the frustration clouded my thoughts for a second, "I just don't know sometimes. Life is happening so fast with me and every time I get an answer to something I realize how much more I don't know. The truth about my family, the truth of angels, or the truth about life in general is all different from what I grew up believing. Dude, you just don't know how confusing it gets for me. Sometimes I don't even know what truth is anymore."

Jason propped himself up slightly. "My dad once told me, that faith begins when there's no sight of the truth. I think there are some things you will discover and there are some things that God will reveal to you. But when you have no answer, when you just don't know that's where your faith comes in to play. Just trust whatever God has put inside you to do."

"Trust God…" I allowed that thought to marinate in my thoughts. That's why I enjoyed hanging out with Jason through college. We had those deep spiritual talks and yet, he was still cool. He could be on the cloud to seventh heaven one moment and be down to earth the next. "Thanks Jason. I'm gonna try to remember that."

"No problem, Andrew. Get some rest and stop snoring."

"I don't snore!" He gave a skeptical look and rolled over on the air mattress pulling the cover over his head. I resituated myself on the couch and rolled over.

"Loopy!" I gasped quietly. Loopy was staring me dead in the face on the arm of the couch. It startled me. "Bad cat, get down!" She jumped down but was acting weird.

"Stupid cat." I think she understood me because she looked backed at me. It was creepy.

The next morning, Christmas eve, I was at the hospital bright and early. Courtney had called me and woke me up and agreed to meet me there early.

"What room is Mackenzie LaRue in?" I asked the receptionist. The hospital wasn't a big one but I didn't want to wander aimlessly looking for my friend.

"Room B12" She said. I was getting chills being in that place. Almost instantaneously my body temperature changed from hot to cold, cold to hot. *Pain shot in my head, then in my arm, then in my stomach. I walked down the hall further and I barely felt like I could walk.* Crap, I was empathically absorbing the pains of patients in the hospital.

"Come on, Andrew, focus," I told myself.

I held on to the wall and closed my eyes pausing to breathe. *I could hear the moans of groans of people around me. I could feel the tears of those who had no relief, the screams of the unconscious fighting to wake up.* "Control," I grunted and gritted my teeth. I took a breath. When I opened my eyes I could've sworn the jewel in the ring I was wearing twinkled a bit. Then the pain was gone. As if it never happened. I exhaled.

B12's door was already half open I walked in. The blinds were shut and only a fluorescent light lit the room. Mack was attached to all types of tubes and a weight of sorrow fell on my heart. I couldn't get rid of this though, because this sorrow belonged to me.

"Mack," I whispered, unsure if he could hear me or not. I opened the blinds on the window to allow the illumination of the sun.

"Andrew?" said a soft voice from the

corner.

"Sophie?" I squinted, adjusting to the sunlight. Sophelia LaRue was Mack's baby sister. She was only about fifteen and it common knowledge throughout the town that she had crush on me. Mack was never too keen about that, always giving her a hard time anytime I would come over. Sophie would be watching from the distance trying to steal a hug or blush and run off when I noticed how mature she was getting.

But today, curled up in the armchair wrapped in the blue cotton blanket wasn't the same jovial little girl I had grown up knowing. No, Sophie had the most solemn worried look on her face that I had ever seen.

"You okay?" I asked her. She wiped the sleep from her face and nodded.

"The doctors can't figure out what's wrong with him. Something about his brain function being low. How does that happen, Drew?"

"I don't know, Sophie." I approached her and nestled her head under my arms. I patted down her dark brown hair.

"I'm scared, Drew. I've prayed for God to heal him but sometimes I get scared that maybe …"

I shushed her gently, "Don't say anymore. God heard you. Trust me. Mack's gonna get through this." I looked over at Mack. He was breathing so heavily and I yearned to hear one of his corny jokes again. The negative thoughts of "what if" tried to penetrate my mind but I shook them off.

She released her hold on me and attended to her brother. She rubbed his forehead and sang a melody under her breath and even though I could barely hear it, it sounded very pretty. I always thought to myself that Sophie should be something more that what our little town had to offer. I grabbed onto Mack's hand. I wanted him to know I was there. I wanted to cry but I it was pointless. I needed to get to business. I needed to find Donyel, I didn't have time to feel sorry. How was I going to find him?

I turned around and looked out the window. The ring glowed once and stopped

"Poor poor Mack. It's a terrible thing to be so helpless." Ibo appeared behind me in some alter consciousness that only I could see.

"He's not helpless as long as I'm here," I replied.

"Oh, but you were the one I was talking about," he whispered in my ear over my shoulder. I shrugged at his chin and he pulled back. "Now, now remember I am the puppet master here." he flicked his hand at Mack who began coughing. Sophie tried to appease her brother's sickness.

"Stop it!"

"Well then you start! You're stalling Andrew Turner! Where is your grandfather?"

I subsided my anger. "If I knew don't you think I would have brought him to you by now? Why can't you understand that?"

Ibo entered my personal space and squared up to me eye to eye. He was only slightly taller than me. "You're an interesting one Andrew Turner. It's amazing in all the centuries, in all the people I'm come across, you're not afraid of me."

"Well you're not the first spirit I've seen, sorry to disappoint you."

He smirked. "Why do you practice so much restraint with your power?"

"I don't know what you're talking about."

"Oh yes, you do. You—you are one who can do whatever you want yet you control

yourself and contain yourself like a wild tiger in a cage. Perhaps it's fear? Yes, that's it...you're afraid. So you try to control what you fear the most. And that's your self." I glared at him and despised his talk. I was attempting to keep him out of my head but he was already there. Nothing was hidden from him and he was acting like a mirror—a talking mirror.

"You're quite annoying," I told him.

"This Amelia; you like her?" He made an apparition of her image appear in the window waving like water in the reflection of the window pane.

"She's not your concern."

"But she is just another example of how you feel helpless to assist her in her...problem." I knew he was speaking about what happened to her when she was a child and how that bothered me so much that her abuser was still out there. *"Andrew Turner you have been given power,*

with my help that's amplified, and you can do whatever your heart desires. Why waste that which God has granted you to have?"

My imagination ran wild but I humored him. "And what is your interest in me; indulging in what I can do?"

"Young Prince, you are the key in helping me get Donyel but it does me ...er it does you no good if you don't know how to fight him. You can't kill an angel you know. They will simply be reborn like a phoenix."

He had my attention and I watched him walk around the room unnoticed by Sophie. (I wasn't sure where he was going to go as technically he was in my mind), "And I suppose you are going to be my teacher?"

"Only your guide, you need to use your powers for something that needs to be done. You want Donyel gone, I want Donyel gone, so I can help you help me. We can join our powers. I can

unlock your potential. You are a powerful one, and you don't even know it." He smiled and turned my direction. *"I can feel some of the things you're feeling. You absorb people's energy, they're memories, their life essence. Even now you still have the memories of Amelia like they're your very own. How do you deal with that burden? How do you deal with knowing things and yet you refuse to do anything about it?"*

"Shut up." *I wanted to block him but he persisted and an uncontrollable anger boiled inside of me, I wasn't sure anymore if it was me or Ibo.*

"But it's the truth Andrew Turner. You have a destiny, that's why you were born. That's why your brother was born. You are God's wrath. Feel the power. Help those who are crying to God for help. That is your duty."

Ibo frustrated me with his constant

ranting, "My duty? What do you know about what I'm supposed to do? You don't know me."

"Oh but I do, young prince. You are not the first and you won't certainly be the last. Humanity has had several chosen ones to fight on the behalf of God and it's quite obvious this is your calling. Your life is one in between worlds; the world of man and the world of the angels. Your angel heritage empowers you to protect humanity and your human blood beckons you to evolve to the very image of the Heavenly Father. Donyel knows that. Eventually, I suppose he would want to control that. As an angel he can go undetected if he has a chosen one as his man of arms."

I looked bewildered. "Undetected by who?"

"The Supreme Government. El Elyon, the God of gods resides at the top of it of course but it breaks down into several hierarchs. It is *through this government that the universal laws are kept. This same government keeps an eye for problems in the creation. Donyel is a rogue, he's doing his own thing. As long as he stays under the radar he's no problem, they won't come after him. If the S.G. gets hint that he's working outside the universal laws then he is liable to be transformed."*

"Transformed?" I asked.

"Yes, he can't be killed but he can be transformed, into something else I'm sure you've read the Greek myths. But that would have to be done by a god. If Donyel does too much to interfere with the order, then his molecules can be transformed into something less harmful, like a tree, a marble statue, or just spread his energy so far it takes a millennia to put himself back together. Such a sad way to go," Ibo said very insincerely, "So I can feel how he wants you. Being human you have free will. You can do

Donyel's will without him getting in trouble. That's how Helel does it."

"*Okay, who is Helel?*"

"*Helel is the leader of the great rebellion, that's not really your concern. But even the outlaws are allowed to be at times because Elyon can purpose them for the order. Chaos and creation go hand in hand after all.*"

"*And you—you were a part of these outlaws?*" *I asked Ibo.*

"*At one point. Now of course, I'm a prisoner of war.*" *He looked around the room.* "*But the war isn't over. It continues with you, however I fear you will lose because when Donyel comes after you, you will not be ready.*"

I thought about what he said and to some extent he was right. I had never confronted Donyel before and just the fear of my parents hiding us all our lives was an indication that perhaps I was biting off more than I could chew. I needed to have a plan to find Donyel and then fight him.

"So what should I do?"

Ibo walked up to me and touched my shoulder like a concerned friend. "Stop resisting. You've been trained your whole life to deny yourself. Subconsciously, you have dwarfed your powers."

"I don't know that I am resisting. I want to use my powers."

"Then let me help. Do you want me help?"

I hesitated.

"Yes."

Ibo smiled. "Good, I thought you'd never ask." He disappeared.

Everything resumed in reality as normal. I felt a surge go up my spine and my hairs on my arms felt like they were standing on end.

"You okay?" Sophie asked. I turned around and smiled. My parent's worse fear was that Donyel would find us.

"Yeah, wow look at the time. It was good seeing you again. A girl named Courtney may be coming by, she knows Mack as well."

Me and my brother were discouraged from using our powers because it was thought it would be a like a spotlight attracting Donyel to us. Now I wanted him. So I knew what to do.

"Okay…" She seemed bewildered. "you didn't want to wait on her?"

"No, I have someone else I need to see today before the day is out."

CHAPTER TEN

Karen made it to the house with Me-ma and together the women wasted no time in preparing the Christmas dinner.

"Where's Courtney and Antonio?" Jason asked.

"Dropped them off at the hospital, Courtney wanted to check on Mack," Karen told Jason who looked as if he was left out the equation.

"I guess I'll just go roam around outside then."

"Oh, baby I can take you over there if you like?"

"No ma'am it's okay," Jason answered. He didn't want to be a nuisance. "Go ahead and finish up your dinner. I can keep myself company. I'm still reading this book."

"Momma Wallace?" Anthony walked in from the bathroom with his arms out petitioning his hug. Me-ma grabbed him so tightly.

"Merry Christmas Anthony, I saw the other baby last night. You've done a good job raising that boy."

"Thank you."

She frowned up her face. "I sho'll wish you and Andrea could've worked out something before she left to the sweet bye and bye."

"Things were too difficult, Momma Wallace, with my job in Dallas and all and her wanting to live here. But I always loved and will love her." Karen sheepishly smiled at his comment. Andrea and Anthony had always told some crazy story about why they couldn't be together to Me-ma but that old woman still knew more than she was letting on. Old people were always like that, a deep well of secrecy known only to them.

She patted his shoulder and continued to tend to the kitchen. Anthony caught Karen's attention and brought her to back room with haste.

"What? What are you doing?" She asked.

"We need to talk about Donyel," he whispered as if he were afraid that somehow Mema could hear through walls.

"Oh no, let's not open that can of worms again. It's Christmas eve."

"We need to have some plan of action though."

"Anthony," Karen whined, "we came down here for you...and the boys; not to do some spiritual warfare. Can't we just have a normal Christmas like a normal family?"

The family thing caught Anthony off guard. He paused wanting to comment but refrained from doing so. "Karen, the only way we can be normal is if we make sure that Donyel isn't interfering in our lives."

She sighed, "But it was just a dream. I don't want to relive all of this again. I mean after what happened to us in college Anthony, fighting Donyel, Tamela, and Philip we practically lost our lives in that house that night. If it weren't for Donyel, Courtney's dad would still be alive."

"I miss Dewayne too, he was my best friend but Donyel hasn't changed. He still has the same agenda, he wants to eliminate any threat to his creating a people that will worship him. Andrea knew that if he couldn't get to her he would try our children."

"About that," Karen interrupted, "Don't you think you should, I dunno, ease up a little on Antonio."

He grunted. "Are we back on that again? Look, I need my son to listen to me."

"Your son," Karen continued, "is a man.

A very special young man and if you give him a chance I think he can prove to you how responsible he is."

"Karen, he's never listened to me. He's just hard-headed. But I don't have time to think about that right now. Look I just need you to pray with me right now that God will strengthen and protect us." Karen felt honored that Anthony invited her to pray with him. Anthony really had no other recourse for action, his fight was spiritual and he wanted to make sure that he had all his bases covered.

Jason was in the backyard. Loopy graced across his leg. He snatched the cat with the quickness. "Show yourself!" he glared at the cat.

Loopy hissed and clawed in his grip. Her head twisted back and forth. *Philips's spirit spurted out like a black milky hair ball and manifested into his normal form. Philip backed into the shadows. "How'd you find me?"*

"I can smell you."

Philip quivered in fear realizing what stood before him. "You're not a human you're.."

"...Shariel." Jason's form morphed into the tall illuminating guardian with long twisted locks of hair floating around him like tentacles. "Demon, bow before my presence!". The light emitting from Shariel practically washed Philip out like the sun at dawn.

Philip bowed. "Please my Lord, don't torment me! I am just doing as I was ordered to do."

Shariel approached Philip. "Did Donyel give you these orders?" Philip nodded. "And what were your orders?"

"If I tell you, he would hurt me! I can't..."

Shariel's eyes glowed like fire. "You should be more afraid of what I can do to you, terrestrial spirit!"

Philip struggled to keep his manifested shape and faded in and out of existence like a bad television reception. "I just-just report what I overhear Holy one, I assure you. It's not me you want. Donyel wants the boy. Shouldn't you go after him? Donyel is probably not far."

"The boy? He's only after one of the twins? Which one does he want Antonio or Andrew?"

"I don't know." *Philip shuttered in the shadows. Shariel flipped his hand and levitated Philip inside a fiery sphere.*

"I don't know!" *the orb ignited more with a twitch of Shariel's lip. Philip screamed in agony,* "Ahhhhhhh! Mercy!"

"There is no mercy for the likes of you." *Shariel declared to Philip spinning him upside down and decreasing the size of the orb as to deform Philip's plausible shape.*

"Are you going to torment me?"

"No," Shariel answered and transformed back into Jason.

"But when I see Donyel, I will let him know who my informant was." He winked and like a twinkling star disappeared. Philip, frantic, dissipated into the wind to find his father.

"Amen," Anthony said finishing his prayer. "I feel somewhat relieved now."

Karen smiled. "Why is that?"

"Well it took God's angels to help us last time, I have faith that wherever they are they are busy working on our behalf."

"Let's hope so," Karen said going back to the kitchen. Anthony's phone rang.

"Hello? Helloooo?" No answer. "Must be a bill collector. Is there no time they won't call?"

"Ya'll were in there for a minute, talking." Me-ma pried trying to get some information from Karen when she came to the kitchen.

"He just wanted to pray about some things."

She looked surprised and made a sound that she was impressed. "Hmph! When a man asks to pray with you that's pretty serious." Me-ma fiddled with some giblets.

Karen shrugged it off. "It was just a prayer."

"Baby, for a spiritual man, a prayer is more intimate than a kiss."

"Oh Mamma Wallace." Karen commenced to wash the dishes. Maybe she thought it would wash away those silly thoughts she was having in her head. It was those thoughts that made her invest so much time in a man that she thought was obviously preoccupied in everything else but her.

But Me-Ma knew. "Karen," Me-Me looked her dead in the eyes and stopped her from washing the dishes. "I know you got feelings for

Anthony. Even if he doesn't realize it, he needs a woman like you in his life. You just keep being there."

Karen shied away from the comment. She didn't want to admit the obvious even to herself. It's strange that even when people know the truth in themselves they still can't confess it. But it's in the confession of the truth that makes it a reality.

"What are you ladies in here whispering about?" Anthony said entering the room.

Karen looked startled. "Oh...nothing." Me-me just looked at them both, smiled and went back to cooking.

CHAPTER ELEVEN

"Andrew said he would meet me here," Courtney said taking her jacket off as they entered the hospital.

"Great. Let's just hurry up, hospitals give me the creeps." Antonio removed his scully cap from his bald head and went to the receptionist. "I'm looking for Mackenzie Larue."

"Hey weren't you here earlier?"

"Heh, no that was my twin brother. Is he still here?"

"Well, I haven't seen him leave and I've been here all day. Mr. Larue is in B12," the receptionist said.

"Thank you." Antonio headed down the hall. "Courtney, I have to ask you something about yesterday."

"Yesterday was crazy," Courtney said as she walked next to him.

"Yeah, but you sensed something was going to happen and something happened. What's up with that?" Antonio jived.

Courtney wasn't quite sure. "I guess that's what kept me away so long. I can't deny that I have some connection with Andrew—I mean your family. When I'm around you guys it like stimulates something inside of me. I start having these weird dreams and déjà vu feelings about what's going to happen."

"So what's wrong with that?" Antonio asked.

"It's one thing to have a special friend but when that starts rubbing off in your own life it gets scary. I never planned to start seeing things but the first time was when Andrew took me to the prom. I had a vision that something bad was going to happen and then I had a bad vibe about Tonya."

Antonio thought for a second. "You ever thought that if you actually focus on this gift that you could get a clear understanding about it? Maybe even control it?"

Courtney stopped walking for a second, every bit of frustration she ever had was about to erupt. "Antonio, no offense but before I met you guys I was just another afro-centric girl in Dallas being talked about because her hair was nappy and needed a perm. That's what made me different. And even though I embraced being different, all I ever wanted in my life was to feel accepted or just be like everyone else. Then I met Andrew and you. And for the first time I was with a group of like minds that made me feel like I belonged. But there was a price attached. Now somehow hanging around you guys has started these visions, and it only happens when I'm around ya'll."

"Like we infected you or something"

"I didn't say that." Courtney didn't want to be misunderstood.

"No it's cool. I understand" Antonio continued to walk

"Antonio it's not like that." It left Courtney a little speechless but she continued, "I have a gift inside me screaming to come out, sparking anytime I'm around you guys. It makes me feel even more different and all I really wanted is a normal life."

Antonio considered everything she said, "But Courtney," he challenged, "what if what you're experiencing is normal? What if people are supposed to be like we are?"

Courtney pondered his statement, then noticed they had arrived to Mack's hospital room. "Drew? What are you doing back so soon?" Sophie looked up from sofa she was lying on.

"No, I'm sorry, I'm Antonio, Andrew's twin brother."

"I didn't know he had a twin." Sophie's eyes twinkled with excitement. For her this was just *"two"* good to be true. Antonio suddenly had a feeling of discomfort at Sophie's star struck gaze.

"Um, yeah." Antonio commented, "Where's my brother?"

"He left like, twenty minutes ago."

"Funny," Courtney said, "the receptionist didn't recall him leaving. Ya think she'd remember a six foot something black guy walking out the door." Courtney giggled. But then, she got that feeling again...the déjà vu.

"Antonio…" She stopped and tried to gain her senses but it was like she was seeing everything playing out in her head. She was watching a movie but it involved all of them.

"Courtney?" Antonio looked at her

concerned and pulled her into the hallway. "let me get you some water."

"I'm okay, just having that strange feeling again." She looked up into the reflection in the circular mirrors in the hallway corners. Visions flashed across her mind constantly as she tried to make sense of what they were trying to tell her. "I think Andrew is in trouble again."

"Man...not again." Antonio's frustration was obvious. "Recently trouble has just been finding this guy."

Courtney shushed him as she tried to focus on the images she was seeing in the mirror. "I see... oh my God! I think he's trying to kill Santa Claus."

"You gotta be kidding me," Antonio said in disbelief.

"No. I think I just had a vision of him with all this power and then like, Santa Clause dying."

"So what's his goal here, is he trying to stop Christmas or something?" Antonio's sarcasm was biting.

"Antonio, we've got to find him!"

Antonio looked confused. "I'm sorry I left my Andrew radar back at the house."

Courtney paced. "You're twins can't you like concentrate or something on him and figure it out?"

"You want me to summon…my brother. You've been watching too much television."

"Well we need to do something! I'm not sure what I saw but whatever it is I think that Andrew is in a lot of trouble." Courtney had genuine concern over what she saw in her vision. Antonio was still skeptical and unsure of what exactly she wanted him to do.

"If you're going to find Andrew you guys are going to need my help," Jason said walking into the hallway.

Antonio jumped. "Man you scared me. I didn't even hear you walk up.". Jason put his hand up to communicate he was focusing. He looked up and around in the air as if he were trying to listen to someone whispering from beyond.

"Andrew, is being influenced by Ibo. He's taking things into his own hands and …" He paused to close his eyes and focus further. "if you don't stop him he will do something he will not easily be able come back from."

"Wait, wait…how do you know all this Jason? Don't tell me you got powers too." Antonio threw his hands up.

Jason simply looked at them both with his true eyes and revealed the truth of his identity without saying a word.

Courtney covered her mouth. "Shariel."

Antonio pointed at him. "You were the angel that saved our lives when Tonya tried to kill us a couple of years ago."

Jason nodded. "Time is wasting. I can find Andrew."

"Well let's go," Courtney said and grabbed Jason's hand and pulled him down the hall. "You can ride with us."

Jason smiled at Courtney impressed at her tenacity to do something. "There's no time. Ibo has used his power to teleport Andrew to his destination. We need to get there now. Your best option is to ride with me." He held on to her hand and touched Antonio's shoulder and looked at him. "You ready?"

Antonio was having difficulty digesting all these new surprises but was learning that with his family anything was possible. "Where are we going?"

"Houston." And with that said they faded from sight.

CHAPTER TWELVE

"I wonder where the kids are. They should've be back by now," Karen said as she looked up at the clock. It was going on three o'clock and all the pre-Christmas munchies were ready for munching.

"I keep calling Antonio's cell but no one's picking up," Anthony mentioned quietly. He didn't want to alarm Me-ma who was sitting in the corner humming and knitting up a sweater or something. It was very cliché for an old woman but she enjoyed making clothes.

"You don't think their up to something do you? I hope Courtney isn't doing something crazy," Karen worried. Anthony was beginning to fume again but calmed himself down to give the benefit of the doubt.

"Maybe their out shopping." Their

attention diverted to the abrupt knock at the rickety front door.

"Knock, knock." Tamela invited herself in.

Karen caught an attitude quick. "What are you doing here?"

"Not here for you my dear, I just wanted to wish Anthony a Merry Christmas. We got off on a bad foot but despite all that's happened we need to put the past in the past." She smiled and offered a cake to Anthony. Karen took it quickly and placed it to side. She didn't trust to eat it, perhaps Tamela was trying to kill them on the sly.

"Thank you very much, I guess you can go now." Karen directed toward the door.

"Wait, let me say my peace." Tamela maneuvered away from Karen's grasp. "I know we all haven't been able to see eye to eye on a lot of issues. But we've all lost someone dear to us in all this craziness. We have a common bond. We've all been hurt and I think we're all just reacting from the circumstances…"

"…the circumstances?" Anthony was in awe. "The circumstance is a fallen angel who I recall you sided with when we were in school, almost killed all of us. The people in our lives that have been lost, have been lost because of that thing."

"He is an angel," Tamela reminded, "Look I was young. I admit some things got out of hand. You know how young people are, we experiment with things; Ouija boards, a séance, whatever."

"I don't remember experimenting with that stuff," Karen added.

"No, you just got yourself pregnant," Tamela bit back.

"Why didn't you tell us that your daughter was the grandchild of Donyel? You deliberately held that secret from us. Knowing about Tonya would have been real important, be that she almost killed my sons."

A slight rouse of anger touched Tamela but she exhaled it out her mouth. "Please, don't spread lies about my daughter. All you have are the words of your sons. My daughter was not born with any powers, the only the thing she knew is what I've taught her and that wasn't much. So what reason would I need to reveal to you about who she is? She was just a normal girl. But your sons; hmm, they are the ones with powers. It's *my* daughter who's in the hospital and the doctors don't know how to diagnose her. It's my daughter whose symptoms change like the wind and who's lost her mind. Who knows? It could be your sons who are the actual killers."

"My son's are not killers."

"Well, I've had a hard time, regardless of who your sons are. We all have special kids. I can't see why we don't get along. Besides it all started with us, right?" Tamela said smugly.

Anthony bit his top lip, "I'm not sure what there is to work on. So much has transpired since college."

"I thought it was Christian to forgive, Anthony," Tamela stated. Anthony looked about. Karen held her tongue in peace and did her best to appear that she was at least trying to be Christian-like so she decided if she couldn't say anything nice not to say anything at all. "If you would excuse me, I think I feel ill." Karen left the room.

Tamela took no offense and sat down on the couch. "Finally, we can talk like we used to without her around."

"There is no used to, Tamela."

"We *did* date, Anthony. Then you changed on me." She stuck out her lip. "There must've been something about me you liked."

Anthony looked at her confused. "What exactly do you want, Tamela? Why are you bringing up the past? I know you're not thinking about…"

"…What? You and me?" She giggled, "Oh, Anthony no! I mean you are still fine as hell though."

Anthony didn't know how to respond. He cleared his throat.

"I'm sorry," she excused herself, "I didn't mean to embarrass you. But I'm very content being a single woman. I just sometimes have a hard time forgiving myself and I didn't want to go through life holding that type of negative energy you see."

Anthony listened to her plea trying to discern her sincerity.

"That's why I came here. It's the holiday season, and I was so mad about you and your family because of what happened to Tonya. Then

I thought that there was so much anger inside because of so many things. That's just not the way to live." She smiled so perfectly and sat with her back straight like perfect southern lady.

"I don't expect you to apologize."

Anthony almost choked on his words. "For what? I've been telling you time and time again. Me and my family are not to blame. It's Donyel, Tamela! He's like a poison to all of us. All he wants to see is us destroyed."

Tamela sat back. "Obviously you don't know Donyel at all. Just like a preacher man. Hmph! You just demonize everything you don't understand don't you?"

Anthony wanted so bad to convince her now, he felt like it was his mission as her very attitude agitated his ego to prove her wrong. "The Bible says test the spirits, Tamela."

"That would be nice, Anthony, but the Bible isn't my book of choice. Just believe what want to, okay? Let's just agree to disagree." Tamela got up from where she was sitting and headed for the door. "I do sometimes wonder what it would have been like, ya know, if it were you and me and not Andrea."

Anthony took the liberty to open the door. "I think you should leave."

"I was leaving *anyways*, thank you very much." She stepped out. "Look, Anthony, deep down I do care about you. Just try to see things my way, Donyel isn't as bad as you make him out to be, you'll see."

"What do you mean you'll see? Have you seen Donyel or something lately?"

She smiled and walked off. It left a bad taste in Anthony's mouth.

"Karen!"

"What?" She ran back out to the den at Anthony's beckon call.

"This is worse than I thought, come on,

let's get to the hospital."

CHAPTER THIRTEEN

I opened my eyes and found myself in a busy mall. People were frantically shopping looking for last minute gifts. I was disoriented for a second but Ibo had teleported me instantly in a corner where no one had seen me. I leaned against the wall. Sweat was dripping down my brow and my heart was palpitating. That little bit of traveling had surged power in me.

"What's happening to me?" I looked at my hands and arms and I could see the blood pulsing through my veins. I felt weak and powerful all at the same time. I was trying to think straight as millions of thoughts and voices swam past through my mind. I brushed past a man and instantly I saw his life; *a lawyer, buying a diamond necklace for his girlfriend and a bottle of perfume for his wife*. I shook my head to clear the thought. Another person bumped into me, and everything in my mind slowed down. *This time a memory of a woman sitting alone in a dark room drinking tea by the fireplace filled my head.* I was sad, or she was sad because once again this Christmas would be the same; no calls, no one caring. I shook my head again to find myself. All these thoughts and memories were jumping in my head instantaneously.

"Control yourself." I saw Ibo in my reflection in a store mirror. "The power is intense and you must gain control of your abilities."

"I don't think I'm ready." I weakly said as I rubbed the temple of my head.

"You control the power, don't let the power control you." Ibo reprimanded. I attempted to compose myself. I needed to focus on what I was trying to do. My plan was still unclear and I wasn't sure if it would work. But Ibo was right, I had all this power and I just sat on it and did nothing but I wouldn't any longer. I wanted to do something, I wanted to bring justice and would start with Cornelius Garrett. I had focused on him and it had brought me to the mall, but finding someone in a mall on Christmas Eve was not going to be an easy task.

    I took a breath and held it. I imagined a bubble around to block out the thoughts of other people. I opened my eyes and I don't know if anyone else could see it but I could see it. An orb of energy surrounded me about two arms length out. For the moment I felt silence in my head but I could faintly hear the hum of this shield I brought around me. I had made one once before but this one seemed far much stronger. It was in fact, so strong that when I walked forward people unconsciously walked around the field. I felt tingly and warm all over my body.

    "Very good, Andrew. Now, focus on him. He is close you must focus on him." Ibo said in my mind and that's what I did. Cornelius Garret, I said in my mind, and I felt like a magnet was pulling me or a wind was blowing at my back. I walked in the direction through the crowd as they made way for me. There in the end of the mall was the Santa's workshop area and a line of kids were waiting to sit on Santa's lap to tell them what they wanted for Christmas. I searched and looked around. Who could he be? Then it was like everyone went it shades of gray and that bright red Santa suit was intensified. I squinted my eyes at how bright red it seemed.

"It's him," I said as everything resumed to it's normal color. Cornelius Garret, the perverted molester who had hurt Amelia so many years ago was now working as Santa. There was nothing more disgusting to me and I wondered how he managed to sneak under the radar without anyone knowing. These poor unsuspecting parents handed their children off one by one to this very sick man. I was a good distance away and under normal circumstances I would have to touch him but my powers were so amplified I merely had to just look into his eyes when he glanced my way and I grasped within myself all manner of memories from him. They flashed in my mind quickly, and I saw Amelia, her pain, her screaming…I turned away and closed my mind. It was too painful.

"Out," I told myself, trying to get the thoughts out my head.

"You okay, son?" an older sales clerk asked me. I was leaned up against a pillar. I nodded and smiled. Being an empath it was becoming harder to let people go, it was hard to forget. I needed to get this guy alone. But the line was all too long and there was no way it would be good to confront him in front of so many people. The opposite use of my power would be to emote how I felt or to emote a thought.

I looked at Cornelius Garrett in his Santa suit and shot a suggestion to his mind. *Go to the bathroom.* I saw him twitch and look uncomfortable in his seat. I repeated the thought. *Go to the bathroom now!* I saw a look of panic hit his face and he whispered something the small elf next to him.

"Sorry kiddies, Santa will be taking a small break," The elf said to the crowd and the parents began to moan and groan. Cornelius snuck off through a back entrance and I went to go follow him. When I entered the men's room Cornelius was just finishing up and washing his hands. I stood behind him watching him through the mirror. I absorbed all the rage of Amelia and children's past. My face flushed and my fist clenched. There he was, the man that had hurt so many, and by feeling their pain in a way I had experienced at well. If I had something in my hand I would have hit him right there. But something kept me from doing so. I needed to make eye contact with him. I wanted him to suffer. I wanted him to know what he did. I had learned so many Christian teachings about forgiveness but right now they were being silenced by the flashes of memories; the cries and pleas of little boys and girls that he showed no mercy echoed in my head. Ibo was right, I was going to be God's hand of vengeance. Perhaps that was my purpose.

"Mr. Garrett," I spoke and he looked up and saw me in the reflection.

"Yes, do I know you?" He turned around and shook his hands dry and grabbed a paper towel.

"You were a teacher right?" I asked, he nodded and tried to see if he could recognize me.

"Were you a student of mine?" He threw

the paper towel away and attempted to fix his beard. "I haven't been a teacher in a while."

"No, I wasn't a student of yours. But I know a student of yours." I walked toward him slowly. "And I'm sure she would like you to know this." I took my right and before he could respond I touched the side of his face. A jolt surged into me as well as him. I used my left hand to grab the other side of his head to hold on. In the past I had done the same with Pastor Francis to find information about my mother's biological mother and almost killed the man. Perhaps this time I could do it on purpose. But in doing so I fell deeper in the mind of this maniac.

I opened my eyes and I was in a hallway. It was a dirty hallway like the type you would see in a dilapidated motel in the trashy part of town. The floors were wooden and creaky and the wallpaper was an old flowery design stained with God knows what. There was rancid smell of cigarette smoke, cheap liquor and urine. I heard crying. It was a child; it was the only sound in the whole place.

"Hello?" I yelled, looking for the child. "Where are you?" I picked up my pace as I could hear I was getting closer. I turned the corner and it seemed the hallway was getting darker and smaller. My head barely grazed the top of the ceiling. At the end of the hallway, a little boy with a bloody, dingy white t-shirt, blue shorts and mangled hair cried huddled in the corner.

"Hey, you okay?" I said approaching him. He flinched and squeezed closer into the corner. "Hey, I'm not going to hurt you. Are you hurt? Where's your mom?"
The little boy pointed down the hall.

I held my hand out. "Well, do you want to go find her? Let's get out of here," I said still holding my hand out. He slowly put his hand out and gripped it tight. He was maybe four or five but he wouldn't talk. As soon as our hands touched, the walls in the hall began to shake and the doors rattled. The knobs twisted and turned and cries from a thousand children from behind the doors screamed and cried. I saw little hands reaching from underneath the space between the door and the floor. The little boy covered his ears and screamed himself. I didn't know what this place was, but it was not a good place. I picked him up and decided to run through the hall. Light bulbs popped as I ran past and planks of wood driven with rusty nails burst through part of the wall to stand as obstacles in my way. I carefully maneuvered around them. The little boy clenched to my neck. All I could see was the exit sign at the end of the hall; that was my goal.

But before I got there, one last door opened and a young woman with ratty blonde hair and a bruised eyes stepped out. She had on a red nightgown with a torn shoulder strap that hung off her shoulder.

She puffed on a cigarette. "What you doing with my kid?" She blew the smoke in my face.

"Your kid?" She had to be kidding. What parent would leave their child in a rundown motel? An even nastier man about age fifty or so walked in the room behind her. She pulled the boy from my arms and made him stand next to her. Before me was the portrait of white trash if I had ever seen it. The man behind her, pacing the room was bald, unshaven, wearing nothing but boxers and a wife-beater that barely covered his belly. He pulled the woman around and forced a kiss on her pulling up her nightgown and exposing her in front of the child. The boy began crying.

"Shut up Cornelius!" The woman said. I stood shocked.

"How much for the kid as well?" The man said.

"No, I don't negotiate my kid!" She pushed the man away. The man pulled at her hair, pulling her head down and slapping her at the same time. "You gonna do what I want hoe!" He grabbed the boy's hair with the other hand. I moved to help but the floor gave in and trapped my foot. The boy screamed. He pulled them both inside and the door slammed. I struggled to get my foot dislodged from the floor. "Noooo! Cornelius!" the woman screamed and cried. The boy screamed a blood curdling cry. My heart pounded and I slammed at the door with my fists. I slammed and slammed pulling on all my strength. The door wouldn't budge.

I let go. Cornelius fell back and slammed on the floor. I simply couldn't do it. I couldn't take this man's life. After viewing through this man's soul who was I to judge what he did? I would be in a non-ending vengeance spree. If I got him then I would have to find who did this to him. Where would it end and then who would I become as a result?

"What are you doing? Why do you hesitate?" Ibo screamed in my mind. Cornelius shivered and sweat poured down his face. He was disoriented and looked around. Could he now hear Ibo as well? I wasn't sure. He looked terrified though. The thoughts I had seen, he had seen as well. I had opened this man's own Pandora's box. He scooted along the floor.

"What are you?" He cried.

"He is pitiful and useless. Look at him! What good is he to anyone or anything in society? You would do this man justice to end his life. Put him out his misery!" Ibo implored.

"This isn't my call, Ibo! You're wanting me to judge this man's life!" I yelled back into the air.

"*His judgment is guilty. I'm wanting you to carry out God's judgment.*" Cornelius wasted no time and picked himself up and ran out the bathroom in a panic.

"My boy, I see you have come into the fullness of your powers," another voice echoed in the bathroom. I looked around and apparently I wasn't alone in the bathroom. I looked in the mirror and far in the corner was the one I had seen in only visions and dreams. It was Donyel.

CHAPTER FORTEEN

"Do you see him anywhere?" Courtney asked. Jason and Antonio looked around the busy mall.

"Come on, angel man, do something. Don't you have like an angel detection device or something?" Antonio pried to Jason.

Jason practically rolled his eyes. "I must have left it back home, Antonio." Courtney smiled a bit at his comment. Jason corrected himself, "I'm trying to focus on Andrew. When I'm not completely in my angel form it's harder, plus I think Andrew is using some sort of cloaking power to hide himself. If he were to focus on something else for a second then perhaps I could find him.

"He has that shield power remember?" Courtney reminded Antonio. Antonio remembered all too much and was trying to forget about it.

"I had one or two run-ins with that shield of Andrew's. When he doesn't want to be bothered, it would just automatically pop up and you could feel the force of it push you back. It usually only happened when he was really upset about something. It wasn't something he could just control though."

"Apparently," Courtney added, "Andrew has figured something out. It must be the ring. Jason, what can you tell us about the ring?"

Jason sighed. "The ring is very powerful. It was created by King Solomon and blessed with the name of God to control the demons and even the angels. After his death the ring was lost and fell into the hands of many men but what they didn't know is that Ibo, the Prince of Jinn was trapped within it. Ibo is subject to the ring and the one wearing it, but he is very clever. He is cunning and makes the ring-wearer feel he is under his control. He makes the person wish for things he wants, then he tortures that person until the person wishes for death, and then he grants that. This has happened countless times and throughout history many powerful men have gotten the ring but it does the same to each one."

"Is that what he wants to do? He wants to destroy Andrew?" Antonio stopped Jason.

Jason looked solemn. "The enemy comes to kill, steal and destroy. He has no other purpose. But my bets are that he has figured your connection with Donyel and that is not good. When he took over Mack's body he was looking for Donyel."

Courtney looked confused. "What does Donyel have to do with this?"

Jason continued, "Before Donyel joined the rebellion he helped King Solomon trap Ibo within the ring. My guess is that there is still some feeling of resentment because of that. Donyel did what he did because Ibo was a rebel angel and Ibo would probably like nothing more than to see Donyel and anyone related to him suffer as well."

"Well great!" Antonio threw his hands up. "That's all I need in my life; my name on the hit list of another rogue angel." Screams stopped the group in their steps. They all ran toward the commotion. Crowds of people gathered while others grabbed their children and covered their eyes. Antonio and Courtney were on the second level of the mall and went over to see what everyone was looking down at.

"Oh my God," Courtney said covering her mouth. Apparently a man dressed in a Santa suit had thrown himself over the balcony onto the lower floor and fallen on his head.

"Someone call the paramedics!" A person screamed. Antonio pulled Courtney away from looking anymore. "Let's find Andrew now!"

"I think I got a read on him," Jason said and started running away from the crowd.

Courtney ran behind them. "You don't think Andrew had anything to do with this do you?"

"God I hope not. I really hope not, Courtney," Antonio said.

CHAPTER FORTY TWO

"Hi my name is Anthony Turner. I was wondering if my sons have come through here. They're twins, taller than me, clean shaven heads, light colored eyes, one has hoops in his ears." Anthony gave a description to the front desk receptionist.

"I haven't seen them leave yet, they should be still up there. But visiting hours will be over in just a few you'll have to hurry," She said and gave the number to Mack's room. Both Karen and Anthony went up but were surprised to see no one there.

"Funny Antonio's car is out there," Anthony said. Karen shrugged and peeked in Mack's room. He was silently sleeping. His heart monitor was the only thing going off.

"Poor kid," Anthony said to himself, "he has nothing to do with this at all." Karen went into the room and looked at his chart.

"Mackenzie *Larue*," She said to herself. She looked concerned.

"What's the matter?" Anthony asked her.

Karen shook her head. "Um, nothing. I don't think. It's just funny that Mackenzie has the same name as…" a scream bellowed from down the hall and then a crash. Anthony looked at Karen and Karen threw the chart down. They both went to the sound.

"This way!" Anthony lead. It wasn't far and the room door was open.

As they looked in, a girl appeared to be trying to get help was on the floor shivering and crying. Her nightgown was drenched in blood and sweat. The blood poured down from her legs and trailed from the bed.

"Omigosh, that's Tonya. Karen, get the

nurse!" Karen grabbed the emergency buzzer on the other side of the bed. It was then she noticed another trail of blood leading away from the bed toward the window. The window was smashed as if something was trying to get out. She looked outside and saw no sign of anything. Anthony grabbed a robe and wrapped Tonya in it and held her head in his lap.

The nurse came in. "What's happening?"

"We need some help! She's losing blood for heaven's sake!" Anthony yelled. The nurse frantically went to grab a close doctor. Karen wasn't sure how much time had transgressed from them walking in. Tonya was starting to convulse. Other doctors had come in by now and Anthony and Karen were made to leave. Soon the whole hospital was on alert.

Karen pulled Anthony to the side. "What happened in there wasn't normal."

Anthony rubbed his head. "Yeah, it's not

what we need right now."

"No, Anthony. That girl was attacked by something and whatever it was escaped out the window."

He didn't want to believe it. "No perhaps you're looking to much into this."

"There was blood on the other side of the bed as well."

"Maybe she busted the window, slid over the bed and fell on the other side," He justified. It was a logical point but Karen still had a feeling in her gut that something wasn't right. The doctor stabilized Tonya's situation but Karen and Anthony stayed to give whatever info they could to what had happened.

Thirty minutes seemed like seconds whenTamela came running in the hallway of the hospital after being contacted. She had a look of panic on her face but when she saw Anthony it changed to rage.

"What are you doing here?" She pushed at him. "Have you done something to my baby!" She pushed him again.

"Tamela! Tamela!" He grabbed her by the shoulders. "You need to calm down. The doctor says Tonya was hemorrhaging blood for some reason."

Tamela looked at the doctor and he nodded at her. Tears filled her eyes.

"Is she going to be okay? What caused this?"

"We're not sure. This usually happens when a woman is having a miscarriage, but that would be impossible since she wasn't pregnant. We're still trying to determine the cause of it. The shock somehow woke her but I'm afraid the trauma of it all has put her back under. We've stopped the blood flow but I'm afraid she's back in a coma."

Tamela buried her face in Anthony's

chest and cried, "Oh my baby!" Anthony held her and allowed her to cry on him. He looked at Karen who thwarted her eyes elsewhere. She kept her peace despite her feelings toward Tamela. This wasn't the time or the place. She managed to sneak out the chaos and go investigate further. She walked outside the building exactly underneath the broken window. She rustled through the thistles and bushes searching for some sort of clue to what had just happened. Behind the hospital was nothing for a wooded forest. It was getting dark so she used the light from her cell phone to assist her. She could hear the cracking of glass under her feet.

"Come on, I need something." She looked around the bushes lighting the area as best she could with her cell. She noticed not only was the glass bloody (which could be very possible given Anthony's view of what happened) but some of the leaves were bloody.

She looked around thinking she heard something behind her in the woods.

"Is someone there?" she asked. "Anthony?" a creepy feeling came over her and she took a small breath to slow her heartbeat. With all that was happening she thought to go back inside. No need to be alone in the dark with fallen angels and demons running a muck. When Karen returned inside she questioned the head doctor that had been working on Tonya.

"Excuse me doctor do you have a moment?" She flashed her badge real quick. "I was just wondering, did the patient have any cuts or bruises on her hand?" The doctor shook his head. "None. If you wondering about the broken window she probably used something to break it."

"Perhaps." She had questioned a lot of people and it seemed the doctor was hiding something but she kept it to herself. Anthony caught up with her in the hall.

"Where'd you go?"

"I needed some air," Karen answered. She didn't have enough information to say anything just yet but something more was going on and she knew it. Anthony's phone rang.

"Andrew? Hello?" No answer. "Hello? Who is this?" He asked. The phone hung up. He checked his caller ID and it was anonymous. "This is getting ridiculous who keeps calling my phone?"

"The question is where are the kids. There's a lot going on and don't feel right not knowing where they are." She called Courtney one more time.

"Hello?" Courtney answered crying.

"Courtney, are you okay? What's wrong?" Karen asked. She had never heard her daughter so scared. Anthony tried to listen in as Karen put her cell on speaker phone.

"Mom, um Andrew...Andrew." She sniffed as if she had been crying.

"What's wrong with Andrew?" Anthony said impatiently.

Courtney tried to compose herself. "Something went terribly wrong."

CHAPTER FORTY THREE

Donyel stood there in front of me. I couldn't believe it. This was my grandfather. This was the infamous fallen angel and he looked no older than me. I would not allow fear to take hold of me. Fear stifles everything inside and I knew if I let it grab hold of me there was no way I would be able to fight against him—if I had to.

"I've been waiting for you, Andrew." Donyel smiled. "You have proven yourself to be strongest of your family and that I can use."

"I don't think so!" I balled my fists and the same shield I used to surround myself expelled from around me in a blast with little effort. The force of it pushed Donyel backwards some but it was little damage than what I had really expected. I should have thought longer about a plan B.

"You are very strong-willed like your mother," Donyel stated.

I didn't enjoy that comment and gave him a second blast just for the sake of it. He laughed it off as if he were enjoying my rage.

"So young and so much to learn. I can teach you so much." He teleported from in front of me to beside me in a blink.

"He wants the ring, Andrew quick!" Ibo whispered. I jumped and somewhat flew from Donyel's grip and floated slowly down onto the bathroom counter. I was hunched like a cat waiting for his next move.

"How long do you think you can resist me, Andrew?" Donyel tilted his head. His long black hair flowed down to one side. "What do you think you are? Do you think you are human? You are of my kind. You are one of the children of the angels." He spun around with his hands out as if to display to an invisible audience. I didn't really care to hear his preaching. "I've watched you. I know you but you don't even know yourself. You want to know your purpose and I know what that is." He held his hand out.

"Release me now, Andrew, and I will fight Donyel for you!" Ibo yelled in my head and this point that was the best plan B I could think of. There was no way I was going to get away from him but if I could distract him for just a little bit I could make my escape. I held my hand out with the ring on it. Antonio, Courtney and Jason came busting in the bathroom.

"Ibo I release you!" I said.

Jason screamed, "No Andrew don't do it!" and morphed quickly into his angelic form. Shariel flew at me as Ibo manifested out the ring in his angelic form. Three angels in one room; it was both beautiful and horrible all at the same time. But suddenly I felt weird. I felt like something was sucking my very breath. I gasped for air and felt my head spinning. I felt my body fall to the ground.

"Andrew!" Courtney screamed. Shariel had pinned Ibo to the wall but in all the commotion and distraction Ibo squirmed out of his grip. He was caught again by the throat by Donyel who was highly upset.

"What have you done?" Donyel fumed.

"Karma," Ibo laughed. Shariel went to my aid holding my body. I could see this but I wasn't in my body anymore. They couldn't see me. But I could neither move close to them or away from them.

"Just like you bound me to the ring," Ibo continued, "Now your heir is bound to the ring as well." In anger Donyel pitched Ibo against the wall that cracked on impact. But then he stopped, smelled the air, "I smell more power in another heir." Donyel laughed. "This isn't over." He directed toward Ibo and faded away.

"Guys can you hear me?" I yelled. But even Shariel didn't respond. Shariel was cradling my head like a baby guarding over my body protectively. Ibo cowered away in a smoky vapor.

Antonio knelt beside me. "Come on Bro, wake up." Shariel transformed back to Jason.

"It's the ring," Jason said, "You can't release a Jinn from its' prison without taking its' place. His soul is somewhere trapped with the ring." That didn't sound good at all. I didn't want to spend my last few youthful years in a supernatural prison. How do I get myself in these messes? The good part, without Ibo I was thinking a lot clearer. But I had no way of getting the message to the rest that I was okay and that we needed to think of something quick. I needed a Plan C. Three times the charm as they say. Courtney was crying and her cell phone went off. She answered it.

"Hello?" it was Karen on the other end. Now would be as good as any to get some parental guidance.

"Mom, um Andrew...Andrew." she sniffed.

"What's wrong with Andrew?" I could hear dad yell from the other end, this was not going to be good. All in all I was trying to stay calm. After all, I was the one trapped and I didn't need to be panicking. Even if I did no one would hear me.

Courtney tried to compose herself. "Something went terribly wrong. Andrew accidentally got his soul sucked into the ring and he's collapsed."

"What!" "Oh God!" I heard both Anthony and Karen scream over the phone.

"Where are you?" Karen yelled.

"Houston." Courtney wiped her tears.

"Wait, how'd you get there?" Anthony interrupted. Courtney spilled the whole beans about the ring, the Jinn and how Jason was really a guardian angel. It was more than I'm sure parents want to hear on Christmas Eve but the shock of it kept them from even thinking about yelling anymore. They both were just in shock.

Jason teleported everyone back to the house in a flash of light. Luckily, Me-ma had already scooted back to her own house or she would've lost her giblets. Still trying to process the information he was just given, Anthony didn't want to get anymore outside parties involved so he laid my body in his bed and Karen wiped my forehead with a wet towel.

"Andrew don't leave us!" Courtney cried. Dad tried to calm her down.

"If only I had got there sooner," I hear Antonio whispered. Courtney rubbed my hand gently allowing the tears on my hand. I felt myself almost floating away and wasn't sure if this was what dying felt like. I had never died before. But I wasn't about to give up that easy.

"We've got to think of something we don't have much time. We can't have Andrew in this state very long. We have Donyel and now what's name…Ibo out there," Courtney said

"Donyel made some comment about smelling some new power in the air or something. Don't know what that means," Antonio commented, "You don't think he's after me next do you?"

"Who's to say?" Jason added, "With Ibo on the loose, he's going to want to strike at any possible person in relation with Donyel." He looked at Courtney as well.

"Why are you looking at me?" Courtney asked.

"Both you and Mack are long

descendants from a bloodline that's connected with Donyel. That's how Andrew can wake up certain gifts within you. That's why you pose a threat."

"All I've had were a few visions. I don't see that as a weapon."

Jason went to the table that she was sitting at in the kitchen, "Your fear and your doubt keeps you from properly growing in your gifts. Once you lose that, you will be able fully develop your potential of your purpose." There was that word again; purpose. It seemed to be ringing in my head this past while. Antonio posed a question as well, "And Mack what can he do? How is he a threat to anybody?"

"Hey, I take offense in that." I heard a voice say. I looked around and there, just as translucent to me and invisible to everyone else was my best buddy as healthy as can be.

"Mack!" I ran to him and gave a hug.

"You're okay! Where were you?

"Sleep. Souls get sleepy too," he joked, *"But here I am waking up and you're here. What happened to Ibo?"*

"I accidentally wished him free and I guess now, I'm the jinn of ring. Wait a minute!" It was all making complete sense now. Mack had gotten imprisoned because of Ibo. Ibo was able to communicate to who ever had the ring on. Now that Ibo was gone perhaps I could free Mack and get the message out to others. Besides, with my knowledge of the history of the ring I think I could devise one more attempt to get out of the ring.

"Uh Drew, you've got that daydream look in your eyes again. It would help to like verbally share your plan with me." Mack waited.

I smirked. This idea was a ray of sunshine on a dark stormy day.

"Sorry, this is what I want you to do."

CHAPTER FORTY FOUR

Courtney walked into the room where my body was laying. Everyone else was still in the living room. She sat next to the bed and gave a burdened sighed. I could sense her presence. I hadn't planned on her coming in but it would be good; I needed her to be able to sense me. If we were going to get Mack back into his own body, we would need Courtney.

"Oh Andrew, I'm so sorry." She sniffed. She was having a moment and I was more curious to how she was feeling. "I feel like this is my fault." No. This isn't your fault. I wanted to tell her that. How could she feel like this? I was the one who had gotten myself in this situation.

"Please wake up. Come back to us," She said. I felt a tear drop on my hand and my soul felt a small pull. Courtney was so special to me. Words couldn't describe how I felt about her. For the life of me I couldn't figure why in our day to day we couldn't see eye to eye. There was a love that I felt between the two of us that was so obvious, so apparent because I could feel it.

She had her hand on mine and I felt like this strong pull on myself. *"Courtney,"* I said and she jumped. She heard me. I knew she did. She looked around the room.

"Andrew?" She looked down at my body and touched my forehead. I needed her to come in contact with the ring though. She sat back down on the edge of the bed. She examined my face and realized that I had not woken up. Her hand was on my bicep by this time. She touched my hand again.

"The ring, Courtney," I said. Her hesitation was obvious. She paused and looked at the ring. Courtney was smart and I knew she

would realize what was happening.

"The ring," She said as if she were having an epiphany. She took it off my finger and held it up so she could see the inscription. It wasn't anything she could read.

"Courtney, you all right in here?" Karen said peeking in. Startled, Courtney spun around placing the ring behind her back.

"Yeah. Wow you scared me."

"Sorry, I was I just checking in on you. Just to see how you're dealing with everything." Karen looked concerned. Just thinking that her only baby was in danger because of distant bloodlines made her nervous.

Courtney brushed her hair behind her ear and smiled. "I'm fine you know you don't have to worry about me. Everything is going to be okay." Karen nodded at her daughter's optimism and walked out the room.

Courtney looked at the ring. "Everything

is going to be okay." She placed the ring on her finger. I felt a rush as if I were being shot through a tunnel. And then everything was still. Courtney opened her eyes and looked around. I think she could feel the power of the ring. She could feel my presence with her. She looked around and into the mirror. She covered her mouth to not scream.

"Andrew!" she gasped.

I was seeing life through her eyes like wearing a mask and she could see me in her reflection. This was a clear result of her gift being amplified by the ring so I doubted that anyone else could see me in her reflection.

"Good I'm glad you can see me," I replied and waved at her.

"Yeah I can see you. Are you okay?" She said touching the mirror.

"As okay, as a guy can feel that's been pulled out his body," I told her. She seemed very

happy and I could feel it. It felt good to be this close to her despite the circumstances. It was like nothing could come in between us.

"Hey Courtney!" that is, except for Mack. Mack made himself appear in Courtney's reflection.

"Mack!" Courtney elated, "I'm so glad to see you're okay as well."

Mack joked, *"Yeah, but I need to get in my own body. Kinda cold being bodiless."*

"Andrew, why don't you get back into your own?" Courtney asked.

"I can't. I'm the jinn of the ring. I can release Mack but in order to get out another has to take my place. Ibo tricked me to release him."

"Not good," Courtney thought out loud, "finding Ibo and getting him back into the ring isn't going to be easy."

"Well let's get Mack free first. Then we'll worry about the rest later," I told her.

Courtney went into the living and room and grabbed Antonio. "Can I speak with you for a second." Antonio didn't have much of a choice. She pulled him outside on the front patio.

"What do you want?" Antonio pulled his arm out of her grip.

"I have Andrew," she whispered and showed him the ring.

"You put the ring…" Courtney quickly shushed Antonio by putting her hand over his mouth.

"Hush! I don't want my mom worrying. And I'm sure your dad wouldn't agree with me putting on the ring after what happened to Andrew."

"Uh, yeah. It makes sense," Antonio sarcastically remarked.

"Andrew's one with the ring, Tonio, and I can hear him and Mack."

"Oh great. So what do we do now?"

Antonio shivered, it was getting colder and colder outside.

"We've got to get to the hospital," Courtney insisted.

Antonio shook his head. "Visiting hours are over I'm sure and there's no way you're going to get to go over there tonight, on Christmas eve without rousing suspicion."

Antonio glared into Courtney's eyes.

"What are you doing?" She reared back. "Trying to see if I see my brother in your eyes," He joked.

She patted his chest. "Okay, backup buddy." She continued to think. "There has to be a way."

A car drove up. "Oh crap," Courtney said.

"What?" Antonio asked and turned to look at the car. Leonard Freeman got out the car.

"Hey Baby, Merry Christmas," Leonard

said, "I thought I come by and drop your present off." She had told him that he was welcome and she knew it. She smiled and hugged his neck.

"Hey Leo!" I cringed at them touching. It was like I was hugging Leonard.

"What's going on?" Mack asked.

"That bonehead Leonard showed up and now Courtney's all cupcakin' with him," I commented with a bit of jealous. I forgot that at the moment my dialogue was pure thought and well, Courtney could hear me.

"Shut up," She said out loud.

"I didn't say anything," Leonard answered.

She laughed it off. "I meant, shut up... you've got to be kidding! You brought my present to me! So sweet of you!" She hugged him again to smooth it over.

"I'm going to be sick," I said. I could hear Mack laughing in the background.

"Hey Leonard. Good seein' ya again," Antonio said trying to be cool with the guy.

Leonard squinted a bit to figure out which twin he was talking to and then realized that he was too cool to be me . "Hey Antonio." They shook cordially but Leonard hesitant because Antonio had whooped on him a couple years ago.

"Hey man it's cool, it's Christmas," Antonio said, "Let's let the past be the past." I was glad Antonio could let go so easily. I, however, had years of bullying from Leonard I had to forgive.

"Man do you always have this much inner dialogue going on?" Mack commented.

"What do you mean?" I replied.

Mack giggled. *"No wonder you write, Bro, you are seriously analyzing this whole situation. I see why you daydream so much Drew."*

"Can we concentrate just a little Mack and stop worrying about me?"

"Can't help it man, your thoughts are pretty loud in the spirit realm."

"I'll try to whisper," I said.

"Thank you," Courtney replied rubbing her head, and then looked at Leonard to justify the comment. "…for um the present you brought me, come inside it's cold out here." They all walked in the house.

Leonard's presence caught everyone off guard. He was the last person they wanted to think about at the moment.

"Everyone, Leonard; Leonard this is my mom and Mr. Turner, Andrew and Antonio's dad," Courtney introduced. I could sense that Courtney was nervous about the whole situation. It was quite awkward.

Leonard noticed a missing face in the group. "Where's Andrew?"

Everyone had the look of the cat that swallowed the canary, "He's not feeling well. He's sleep," Anthony said.

"I'm Jason, Andrew's friend," Jason introduced himself to Leonard then looked at Courtney and froze. I could sense that Jason knew I was with Courtney. Besides he was my guardian angel, it was his job to detect my presence. Courtney gave Jason a fake smile.

Karen tried to smooth the tension. "Well Merry Christmas, Leonard it's good seeing you. Here, I'll get you some tea to warm you up." She went to the kitchen area and began warming up some water. Courtney sat with Leonard by the couch next to the tree. Anthony was sitting at the table obviously very stressed about all that was going on. Karen observed this and patted his shoulder with her hand. He got up and went in the bedroom where my body slept and closed the door behind him.

Jason nudged Antonio. "Maybe you should go talk to your dad."

Antonio whispered back, "You're the angel, you go console him."

Jason showed his disappointment and grabbed his arm and pulled Antonio to the room. Antonio felt like he was being pulled left and right.

"Oh those guys." Courtney giggled and patted on Leonard's lap.

"Um did I come at a bad time?" Leonard said noticing the bit of tension in the air.

"Yes," I said. "No," Courtney said simultaneously. I sighed. Too bad Leonard couldn't hear me.

Karen came into the den area and handed Leonard a steamy mug, "Here you go, Honey."

"Thank you, Ma'am," Leonard replied showing his southern manners and took a sip. I was surprised at how polite he was, how gentleman like he was. This was a side I had never seen of Leonard. This was a side that Courtney knew. Could she feel my jealousy? My discomfort? I was an empath and able to feel others and yet it also allowed me to emote feelings. Were my feelings of discomfort affecting her as well?

Karen sat on the arm of the chair. "You probably haven't heard yet, but um when we were visiting Mack, something happened to Tonya."

Leonard perked up. "What? What happened?"

"Something.." Karen chose her words carefully. "happened and she began bleeding out in the hospital but they've stabilized her. I'm not sure but it looks like someone was in her room before it happened." Courtney froze once again, in shock over the news but Leonard didn't notice because he was in shock as well.

"Well I see why everyone is on edge,"

Leonard said, "especially during this time of year, two of our school friends in the hospital." I could sense that Leonard was slightly more hurt to hear about Tonya and because I felt it Courtney felt it. He was looking into nothing thinking intensely. He took a sip. Karen rubbed Courtney's hair and that's when *I got a flash of what Karen had just said. I saw the memory as if it was my own.* Courtney got the residual view from the flashback. "Well I am going to go check on Anthony. So if you guys will excuse me," Karen said getting up and going to bedroom.

Leonard scooted a little bit closer to Courtney and wrapped his arm around her. At this point I just felt awkward. It was like I was some kind of peeping tom but I didn't have a choice. I was viewing life through Courtney's eyes and feeling what she was feeling and yet I wasn't oblivious to my own feelings, talk about torn. Not to mention I wasn't sure what type of affect it was having on her. Perhaps it was something like being pregnant with child instead the child is practically an adult.

    I thought about the conversations that I had with Courtney about Leonard and seeing this side of him, this sensitive side, just didn't seem right. I didn't trust the guy to say the least. Yeah he was all soft spoken now. But I knew deep down he was just another muscle stacked, meat-headed caveman. In fact, I felt that somewhere the evolutionary chain forgot to include Leonard Freeman. He substituted brains for brawn but I guess all that testosterone was someone attractive to females. Okay, I was somewhat jealous. But in my eyes, Courtney was just too good of a girl to be wasting her time on Leonard.

    I knew it was a matter of time before all that aggression would spill over into some unexpected rage. I was just waiting for it. But no, with her, he was this gentle subtle type. I tried to understand Leonard, really I did, but every time I looked at him I recalled every memory on how he did me wrong for no reason at all. How he teased me and made me feel like I wasn't worth two cents. And for what; what did I ever do to Leonard?

"Leonard baby, can you excuse me I need to go to the bathroom real quick," Courtney said. Leonard kissed her on the cheek.

"Don't be long," he said. She blushed and rushed off. Entering the bathroom she looked in the mirror and we saw each other.

"What is your problem?" Courtney reprimanded.

"*What?*" I said, on the defense.

"You are so upset and jealous. I can feel you throbbing in my mind."

I blew off the statement and gave her my "whatever" look.

"I am not jealous. You can do what you want to," I told her. Courtney paced the bathroom and then tried taking the ring off. It wouldn't budge. Perhaps it was because I didn't want to let go, not yet. Something in me was holding on to her and I didn't want her to pull away.

"Hey I'm sorry don't be mad. Look, I'll try to calm down but you know how I feel about ...him."

Courtney leaned forward on the countertop and gazed in the mirror. "Yeah, Andrew I'm not doing this to hurt you really I'm not. He's my boyfriend and that's just the way it is."

"Yeah yeah, I know," I said nonchalantly. I don't know what I was tripping about. It wasn't like I wasn't dating anybody.

"You're dating somebody?" Courtney asked and I felt a tinge of her jealousy. Perfect.

But then it was swallowed up by some other emotionally mask. "Well I'm happy for you. What's her name?"

"*Amelia.*" And I thought about all that had transpired because of my feelings for Amelia. All that I was willing to do to help her flashed across my mind. Those memories flashed through Courtney.

"You're dating a white girl?" Her tone changed. Courtney was still the pro-black girl that I had first met and I felt a speech coming on that there were too many single black queens out there looking for a good black man for me to squandering off dating outside my race. That was just how she was raised. There was that urge within her to give me this speech but she refrained. Besides, she didn't have to say it I felt it. She tuned into me like radio a station.

"That's the reason you were in Houston." She paused. "Because of her. You were trying to avenge what happened to Amelia."

I couldn't hide anything from her in this state. I was like an open book. Somehow it was becoming all clear to her. "Now I understand." She nodded.

"Well I don't understand any of this. What exactly is going on?" Mack interrupted, "*What exactly is an Ibo anyways again and why is he after us?*"

"Mack, from what I'm putting together from the visions I've seen so far Ibo wants revenge on Donyel and I guess anybody related to him; which includes all of you guys."

Mack seemed confused. "*How am I related? He's your grandfather not mine.*"

Courtney tried to fill Mack in on a small history lesson because he obviously didn't read my book "Heaven Bound" that I based on my family tree and explained all of how Donyel had tried to create his super race of children once in the 1800's (that's the short version). The Larue's, and Courtney's family were of some descent of that family line that ended up revolting. After explaining all this to Mack, it was about as clear as mud but I think he was caught up enough.

"I just wanna know why don't I have any powers or anything. I mean Courtney can see the future and crap in mirrors. I wanna do something!"

"Maybe the powers skip generations," Courtney joked. She attempted to see past our images to her own reflection to fix her hair in the mirror.

Mack commented back, *"Ha ha. Funny, I knew I had to have some black folks in my family. Does this mean I can get considered for an African American scholarship now?"*

"A mind is a terrible thing to waste, but I think yours is wasted away so I don't think they'll be offering you too much. Now hush, I don't need you guys whispering all in my head while I'm with Leonard," Courtney commanded and went back into the living room.

    When she walked out the bathroom, the door to the bedroom was cracked. Courtney peeked in. My dad was sobbing.

CHAPTER FORTY FIVE

Anthony was there kneeling by the bed holding my hand. Karen sat patiently by the dresser.

"I don't think I can go through this again, Karen," he said. Karen tried to compose herself.

"We did it before, we can get through it now .All these battles are to make us stronger people."

He was frustrated. "I lost my wife, one of my closest friends, and now my son?" He looked up at her. "I didn't ask for this. I was just going to be a preacher. That's what I was raised to do. I've lived a life isolated for so long away from my family, separating my present family all so that they could be safe. And still. STILL!" He slammed his fist on the bed. "I couldn't save them."

Karen went to his side and looked into his eyes. "You can't be God to your children. Things are going to happen that we may not be ready for but we have to keep on fighting because whatever's out there isn't going to stop until we are beaten down. Now if Andrea was still here I'm sure she'd have some strong soldier-like words to say because that's what she was, tough. And we have to be that. We've gone through hell but I look at it like this, Anthony...we got through it, and we'll get through this." She hugged him. "Andrew's not gone yet."

Anthony tried to get himself together. "Two angelic beings." He sighed and rubbed his bald head. "This is so unreal, so unheard of. Nothing has prepared me for this."

Karen tried to give a word. "He doesn't give us more than we can handle. When we were in college we fought an angel and his demon-possessed son. We can fight this Anthony."

"That's the thing. We, Andrea and I, just wanted our boys to have a normal life; to live as normal as possible and to be able to have a life outside of all this." Anthony paused in thought, and shook his head.

"But," Karen interjected, "they are gifted. They are above normal. And no matter how hard you try, no matter how they try to fit in with the "norm", they will always find themselves standing out. It's time you accept that and cultivate that. Besides, what is normal other than a setting on a washing machine?"

Anthony nodded and agreed to some degree. He stood up and went to the dresser and looked at a picture of the woman he loved at a time. He sighed, "Sometimes, Karen you sacrifice so much and struggle so much you don't want to see your children go through the same thing. I'm afraid that..."

She put her hand up like a cop halting traffic. "Your fears aren't going to stop anything from happening. They'll just make things worse and then your boys will repeat history. We can't allow our fears to motivate us or keep us from doing anything; either way is bad. The only thing that should empower us is love and our faith."

He smiled because he knew she was right and he felt blessed to have a friend like her. "I thought I was the preacher." Anthony said smugly. Karen smiled to herself and looked down. Even she was surprised at her ability to be so inspirational during this time.

"I've really tried hard to not put my insecurities on Courtney. And even though sometimes I see how she is like me in the bad ways I can't control her. I have to let her learn for herself. But anyhow, what are we going to do about these angels?"

Anthony contemplated a plan. "Hmm, well last time we got Donyel to break a universal law and step out of his bounds so the good angels intervened and trapped him in the third heaven dimension. Maybe we can get him back there again?"

"Yeah but we have two this time and I doubt if Donyel makes the same mistake twice. Plus he has Tamela to do his dirty work now and God knows who else."

"Well, Ibo was trapped in the ring so there's another option. I need to find out more about this ring." He paced the floor trying to think of an idea.

"Well, I'm sure the kids know plenty, I'll get Courtney to fill us in on anything she's figured out. She's pretty much a wiz on studying up on this. So we can..." Karen looked down at the bed. "Uh, Anthony, there's no ring on Andrew's finger." She looked up at him in horror.

"What?" He walked over back to the bedside. "But if the ring isn't on Andrew, then who has it?"

CHAPTER FORTY SIX

"What is your deal?" Jason confronted Antonio in the other room. Antonio was being his normal self he thought. Not really giving a care what anybody thought on the situation. Antonio just simply didn't like being forced into any situation. Antonio was in the room that had once been mine and was now turned into library of old books. The walls were covered with shelves of books and even in front of those shelves boxes of more books. It smelled like old paper and cardboard.

Antonio sat on one of the cardboard boxes and pretended to occupy his time by tying his shoe. "Let me get this straight," he said loosening the knot and retying it, "all this time you've been an angel in our lives, at school with us, and you've been coming over eating up my food. You're an angel why are you eating?"

Jason sighed. "You're trying to change the subject."

"No, I'm asking a legitimate question here," Antonio remarked back.

"Why aren't you trying to help your family when they need you?"

Antonio put his foot down. "And once again I'm saying that you are the angel. You do it." He poked Jason in the chest.

"Antonio, there is much to your calling that you deny and until you..."

"I deny? No, I think my dad has that down, that's his job. And why are you worried about my calling anyhow? I think everyone's figured out by now that Andrew is the good twin that's chosen to do something special in the world."

Jason pulled over a pile of books and sat

across Antonio in the dimly lit room. "Actually you both have a special calling but that's separate yet works together. But just like Andrew, you have to prepare your mind to accept that plan in order for it to come to pass."

"Jason, things are happening without me trying. Nothing is dependent on my decision. Nothing changes and I can't change it. It'll happen regardless." Antonio head dropped some as his thoughts took over. "All my life I've tried to be the best I could be. And it was never enough. My dad just wouldn't notice. I make good grades but it didn't matter. I did well in sports and it didn't matter. You know what I got? Criticism when I messed up. My dad never called me special." He paused, "I was just different."

Antonio shook his head and laughed it off. "different can be so demeaning if you think about it."

"Or beautiful, if you see it's our differences that make us special." Jason added. Antonio let the words seep into his heart a bit but toughened back up.

"I got used to being different though in a bad way. I learned to cope until well, Andrew came along. Then..."

"You didn't feel so different?" Jason completed.

Antonio smiled a bit. "I guess not. But it messed everything up. I don't know how to be accepted. I don't know how to be special. I know how to be different and that's it."

"Life is about learning, Antonio. If you stop learning then you're not growing."

"I don't know what I want really. It's just so much to take in sometimes," Antonio vented, "My dad has just honestly, really not appreciated me like I've wanted him to. And then he puts Andrew on this pedestal like he's heaven sent or something. And I think to myself why do I need to even try?" He stood up and pushed some books off the window sill so he could rest his arms and look out the window. "Don't get me wrong. I love having a brother. I love Andrew." He bit his upper lip. "I love my dad. But when you wanted me to I guess, console him. You wanted me to help and encourage him." He turned around and faced Jason. "How can I? How can I give someone something that wasn't never given to me?"

Jason was a just an angel. Being that, in an angelic state it was hard for him to understand people at times but the longer angels stayed manifested as people the more connected they felt to their emotions. Jason for a second felt this pain that Antonio expressed and even he stopped to think. He stood up. "Antonio, as one of your family's guardians there is nothing we haven't seen you go through. But I assure you every good thing and every bad thing is for your growth. A flower needs both rain and sunshine to grow."

"I'm a not a flower."

"But you get my point. You and your dad share some of the same pains. A part of the reason you don't get along so much is that because you're so much alike. So in truth, you've always had someone like you all along. You were never different. You wanted someone to relate to and you already had it. What you wanted you already had and that was in your father."

Antonio tried to walk past but Jason caught him by the arm and even with his strength there was no getting away from Jason's power grip. "Your dad does love you, Antonio. He is not perfect. I don't think any parent is. Remember they are just young children themselves all grown up, still trying to figure out life like you. And after all the lessons they've taught you sometimes the best things they learn are through you."

Antonio relaxed a bit and in a softer tone he said, "So what's up with my calling? What exactly am I supposed to be doing?" Jason smiled at his response.

Jason patted him on the back and looked into his eyes. "When the student is ready, the teacher will come. Your mission is one of love. That's what you truly desire isn't it?"

"Uh, so what's that mean? Man you gonna have to stop with all the mysterious talk and make it plain. I ain't no lil white boy named, Harry Potter."

Jason laughed. "Plainly said, have patience, your guardian I'm sure will help you figure it all out."

"I thought you were my guardian angel?" Antonio asked.

"No, I the guardian over your family and personal guardian over Andrew."

"So where's mine?" Antonio asked, spooked.

"He's here, everyone has one. I see them all and they all help out every now and then but do their best to not interfere but when it's time, because you are special, he will reveal himself to help you, just as I have done."

Antonio felt a little even more creeped out by the answer but it gave him something to look forward to. For the first time he felt like there was something special about his life, that he had a purpose.

"Things happen that are meant to happen. But you just keep doing and striving to become what you know God has whispered into your heart," Jason encouraged.

Antonio smiled. "I'm still having difficulty hearing that whisper." Antonio heard

Courtney's name being yelled so both him and Jason left the room.

"What's wrong?" Antonio asked. Anthony and Karen were in the living room.

"Where is Courtney?" Karen asked frantically. Antonio shrugged his shoulders. The house wasn't that big and she couldn't be that hard to find.

"Do you know where the ring is that was on Andrew?" Anthony said in a fatherly voice at Antonio. After all the talk, Antonio felt the need to get on the defense again because at the way his dad came at him with the question. But Jason gave him a silent look and Antonio kept his peace.

"Yes, Courtney has the ring." There was no need to lie. Antonio thought it was a dumb idea for her to have it anyways, "But for the record, I didn't think..."

"Why didn't you tell us! After what

happened to Mack, and what happened to Andrew!" Anthony yelled. Karen pulled him back.

"Come on," Karen said, "we don't need that right now." Anthony walked away and paced the den area and then over to the kitchen while he rubbed the space between his eyes.

Antonio sighed.

Karen went over to Jason. "So you're an angel. Can you possibly detect where Courtney has gone?"

"Yes, just give me a moment." He focused and closed his eyes. A flash of thoughts crossed his mind and his eyes popped open.

"This isn't good."

"What?" Karen said.

"I'm getting static, last time that happened, Ibo was blocking me out."

"Ibo?" Anthony stopped pacing, "meaning what exactly?"

Jason looked around. "He's very close to Courtney right now."

CHAPTER FORTY SEVEN

"Are you sure you want to spend the night at my place?" Leonard said as they drove away in his car.

Courtney looked out the rear view window back at the house she was leaving behind. "Yeah" She was trying to control her breath. "It's so crowded there and I would like to spend some more time with you. I'll call my mom from your house." She had left so quick she had forgotten her cell phone. She overheard her mother's conversation with Anthony and realized they had discovered the ring gone. It was an immature thing to do surely, but she was sticking with the plan. It had to work. We would put Mack's soul back into his body.

"Listen, Heaven Hospital is not like a

normal hospital, it's small and country. Even though it's late we should be still able to get in there. People spend the night with their loved ones all the time," I told her.

"Can we stop by the hospital real quick?" Courtney suggested.

"Sure, sure. What seems to be the problem?" Leonard asked.

"I just want to check on Mack real quick," Courtney said.

"I find it real interesting how you've managed to connect so well with everyone from Heaven being that you are primarily an outsider."

"Yeah well, it's like we're all connected in some way that I just can't deny."

"Tell me about it," Mack commented in thought. The car zoomed by house after house on the road and it was fortunate that most people were already home with their families on this

Christmas Eve.

Memories of my mother's car accident flashed in my mind, *"He's going awfully fast isn't he?"* I said.

"Nice ring, where'd you get it?" Leonard asked. Courtney covered up her hand.

"Oh, um, it was a gift?"

"From Andrew?" He asked. His voice was condescending.

"What?"

He sped up. "Don't lie. That wouldn't be good."

"This isn't good," I said.

"What's not good?" Courtney asked.

"I think that Andrew gave you that ring."

She tried to laugh it off. "What? No Leo, you are trippin'." She pulled down the vanity mirror to fix her hair.

Leonard touched her hand. "Let me look at it." When he touched her the combination of my power and hers and the amplification of the ring showed her something in the mirror. In the reflection she saw Ibo driving the car over a ledge with her in it!

She slammed the mirror back to its closed position and pulled her hand back.

"Did you just see what I saw?" I asked.

"Is there a problem?" Leonard asked

"Yes," Courtney answered; to whom I wasn't sure but by her reaction it was quite obvious she was nervous now.

"That's not Leonard," Courtney thought back to me, *"It's Ibo!"*

"Okay try to calm down," I said.

"Calm down, you seem nervous," Leonard said to her.

"I'm calm," Courtney smiled.

"Why wont you let me see the ring?"

"Why are you driving so fast?" Courtney gripped her seatbelt and with the other hand the door handle.

"Is there a problem?"

"I would think so. Angels who commit a murder on a human would be breaking a universal law of interference. That could get you in a lot of trouble," Courtney revealed.

Ibo revealed himself and shape-shifted to his true form. His wild hair and cunning smile seemed even more sinister in the illumination of the car interior lights. "Aw smart girl, there's no fooling you. But would this be murder..." He swerved crazily to another part of the road and was headed to the outskirts of town. Dust and dirt skidded from behind the car. Courtney gasped.

"You can always jump out." He thrusted his hand past her and the passenger door ripped off the car tumbling across a field. Courtney screamed as the landscape flew by so quickly and the gusts of wind blew across her face.

Ibo laughed and hopped in his seat. "Just an accident! Only an accident!"

My own heart dropped as I thought about losing Courtney and there was no way I was going to let that happen. I could hear Mack screaming in my thoughts as well. *"We are one Courtney. What I can do, you can do. I won't let anything happen to you."*

She nodded that she could hear me and she understood. Ibo laughed, "Give me the ring! Or I will pull it off your dead body!" We were traveling on a dirt road by now and approaching an old bridge way to old for car travel and underneath it a cold river that flowed on the outskirts of Heaven Texas. It was his intention to drive the car over the bridge into the river. I wouldn't allow fear to overcome me as I thought about how this was the exact way I lost my mother. Karen was right, I had to focus on the love I had and not the fear. I'm glad I had heard that. Seconds seemed like forever as it no longer seemed like Courtney was in the car but my self. She was in the car, but now I was in the driver seat figuratively speaking, I was taking control.

"Do you trust me?" I asked.

"What?" She thought back.

"Jump out the car," I said.

"What!" Mack responded.

"Jump out the car Courtney. I love you, I got you! Trust me!"

There wasn't much time to think it over but I could tell a whirlwind of contemplation transpired in her mind in milliseconds but logic no longer mattered. Her school knowledge no longer mattered. All that mattered was that deep down she knew I wouldn't let her down.

She snatched the seat belt off and sat up in the seat. Ibo was trying to grab at her hand with the ring while speeding toward the bridge. Her head was out the door and the wind was blowing her hair wildly. The cold air whipped across her face. I closed my eyes. She closed her eyes. Mack closed his eyes.

We let go. The wind caught us like a kite and I flew out and up into the air. Or Courtney was flying up and into the air with *my* power. Her arms were spread out and the wind flapped her shirt around her. She floated higher up and behind the car in the night sky. "Oh my God," she said opening her eyes, "Andrew I'm flying!"

I think she could feel my presence holding her because that's how I imagined it in my mind. I was holding her tight lifting her away from danger. And perhaps my spirit was doing just that. But all that could be seen was her and the car Ibo was driving, falling into the shallow river.

Courtney floated down effortlessly. She knelt on the ground trying to catch her breath.

"Everyone okay?" She asked.

"Yeah." Mack answered weakly.

"You okay," I asked back concerned. She nodded. Then we heard metal being ripped as Ibo was fighting his way out the floating car.

"Oh no," Courtney said as looked around. She was in an empty field.

"Go!" I said. Courtney started running back toward the road. A motorcyclist zoomed by.

"Get on, quick!" the stranger said. Courtney stopped short, not sure what to do. I tried a quick empathetic scan and I sensed no angelic being in this person but still I wasn't close enough to tell.

"What do you think?" Courtney whispered.

"Right now, I would go and ask questions later," I suggested. Courtney jumped on the back of the motorcycle and the cyclist zoomed away.

CHAPTER FORTY EIGHT

"You promised me!" Tamela screamed within the circle she had cast. Donyel stood before her with a solemn holy look of an angel. Looking nothing like his normal sinister self but appearing somewhat sympathetic.

"You promised me she wouldn't get hurt. That you would bring my daughter back to me!" Tamela growled and pointed accusingly.

Donyel's long black hair was split down the middle and his hair fell down over his shoulders. He was wearing a long trench that was caped over his naked shoulders.

"Many connected to me are under attack. I can only be in a few places at a time. But I must protect those who show the most potential." He opened the jacket. A small girl no more than two with blood stained cheeks and hair gripped his white long fingers. She had the most remarkable hazel eyes and she had a full head of curly brown hair that made her resemble a dandelion.

"Who is this?" Tamela said wiping her face.

"She is yours. I need you to watch over her and raise her in my ways. Protect her from the spirits that might try to do harm to her and society that wouldn't understand her. Home school her, and teach her. You won't have long and must do this quickly for she is very, very unique. In fact, I think she is the key."

"The key? What are you talking about? What about my daughter?" Tamela asked.

"In time I will tell you all that you need to know. But in order for you to get what you want, I must get what I want and a part of that is for you to raise this little girl as if she were your daughter." Donyel directed the child toward Tamela.

"Don't be scared," he told the child and he slowly began fading away.

"Wait where are you going?" Tamela reached out.

"I won't be far. I need to visit an old acquaintance that I met some years ago." With that said, Donyel faded away. The child seemed harmless but yet there was something enchanting about her. Something that Tamela couldn't put her finger on.

The child smiled and it reminded her of how Tonya smiled. She took the naked child into her arms.

"Come now, let's find you some clothes so you don't catch a cold. Would you like that...hm." Tamela paused. "He didn't tell me your name." She looked at the child's crystal-like eyes which were like jewels. "Well I will just have to give you a name and I know exactly what to call you." Tamela kissed the little girl.

CHAPTER FORTY NINE

The cyclist zoomed back into the town square. "Stop here I need to do something," Courtney yelled so that the cyclist could hear her.

The cyclist parked the bike by a curb. Courtney got off the bike to see her knight in black leather pants and a blue biker jacket. The biker got off the bike as well and removed his helmet. But he...was a she.

"You're a girl!" Courtney observed.

"Last time I checked, yeah." Her voice had a familiar soft sarcastic tone. She looked somewhat Indian, but not in the native American way. Her hair was dark and wavy and fell slightly below her chin. She wasn't old at all. She couldn't be any more than seventeen.

"Hey, I'm Haadiya." She offered her hand and gave Courtney a strong manly shake.

"I'm Courtney. Um thanks for giving me a ride back there. My boyfriend uhh I guess.." Courtney searched for an explanation.

"Evil angel? Don't worry about it," Haadiya stated as if it was all in a days work for her.

"Wait, what?" Courtney was thrown off course for a second, "How do you know?"

"I was sent," Haadiya said looking at Courtney very seriously, "here to Heaven, Texas to help."

"You're not an angel are you?" Courtney was trying to clarify.

"No, look, I'm human just like you. But I know what's going on and I can help. Now we can sit here and ask questions all day or wait for that angel to get back at you." She started to get back on her bike.

"Wait I need to go to the hospital. Walk and talk." Courtney wasn't near through. Haadiya followed Courtney to the nearby hospital in the town square taking her backpack with her.

"What's at the hospital?" Haadiya asked.

"A friend. But you answer my questions first. How do you know about the angels?"

Haadiya pulled two books out her bag; one was Heaven Sent and the other was Heaven Bound, "I think you guys make it quite obvious. But I guess the best secrets are best kept out in the open. Art imitating life is quite genius."

Courtney tried to play it off. "Those are just books, fiction, they aren't real."

Haadiya walked briskly next to Courtney. "Sure, if you say so. All our lives are just stories waiting to be written. Maybe yours just seems like fiction because it's so abnormal but the supernatural world is more real than any romance novel." She laughed, "Look you don't have to fake with me. I know, I was sent here to help."

"But by who?" Courtney insisted.

"I will explain it all when I see Andrew."

"That may be a little difficult," Courtney said.

"Why is that?"

Courtney raised her hand to Haadiya, "Because of..."

"Oh my God, is that Solomon's ring?" Haadiya perked up and tried to look closer.

"You know about this too?" Courtney pulled her hand back not sure to trust the girl yet. She could be some one who could help or some crazy chick from a book club that had taken reading to a more proactive level.

"Well I've heard stories about it, my mother..." She paused. Something bothered her. "used to tell me these old stories when I was a girl. And then I've done some studies on it myself. I knew it was supposed to find you but I didn't know this soon. Wow I'm behind, we have to hurry then."

"Find me?" Courtney asked reaching the hospital and lowering her voice to a whisper.

"Not you per say. The family, Andrew and Antonio." The two girls made their way through the hall and to Mack's room where his body was fighting for life. It was good that his family had not yet given up on him.

"Is that Mack?" Haadiya asked, "what happened to him?" Frustrated that Haadiya knew so much she blocked her from coming into the room.

"I'm not answering any more questions until you start spilling the beans sister."

"It's complicated and from the looks of it I don't have much time. But I promise you that I will explain every thing. Including on how to fight the Jinn." Courtney eased up and let her come in. They closed the door quietly as to not alarm the one or two attendants walking around. Courtney placed the hand with the ring on Mack's forehead and the jewel in the ring glowed.

Mack gasped. "Whoa, feels good to be back."

"Thank God it worked!" Courtney hugged Mack.

Mack laughed. "Aww see don't hug a brotha too tight, I might get excited."

Courtney punched Mack playfully.

"Wait, so if you have that much control over the ring, then you've must've released the Jinn of the ring. But someone has to take the Jinn's place," Haadiya deduced.

"Yeah, that's the problem." Courtney crossed her arms. "Good ol Andrew's problem actually."

Mack tried to get up but groaned in pain.

"Rest Mack, your body has been sitting for a minute," Courtney suggested and focused her attention back on Haadiya.

"I'm trying to get a read on her but she seems to be blocking me out somehow," I told Courtney.

"Andrew is a part of the ring now. We need to figure a way to get him out safely," Courtney said.

"Some other spirit of great power would have to take his place," Haadiya mentioned. This was all common knowledge by this time. "But I think I may have a plan."

"What exactly is this plan?" A voice said from the hallway. Anthony walked into the room not looking very happy.

"Mr. Turner!" Courtney said as her mother walked into the room, "How did you..." Courtney stopped mid sentence as Antonio walked in behind him.

"Jason was kind enough to teleport us here," Antonio said.

"Courtney you know your mother is back at the house worried sick," Anthony said. He left Karen to watch over my body and Jason was there to watch over her.

"Who is this?" He asked directing his attention to Haadiya.

"I'm still trying to figure that out," Courtney answered, "But she saved my life from Ibo." Courtney rubbed Mack's hand.

"Yeah, Mr. T, I think she's cool," Mack vouched.

Anthony stepped up to her and Haadiya's whole demeanor changed. She seemed to be uneasy and nervous. "Where are you from and how old are you? You don't seem like you're old enough to be out fighting angels."

"Last time I checked there wasn't an age requirement. In a war, we all become soldiers,"

Haadiya said so distinctly.

"You didn't answer my other question," Anthony probed.

"I grew up on the road. Like I told Courtney I'm here to help. I think I have an idea. Someone has to replace Andrew in the ring or he will never get out and that pretty much has to be willingly. After that, you have to figure a way to trap Ibo back in the ring and that's going to take everyone's help."

Anthony was skeptical. "You still haven't told..."

"Look, you can debate who I am all night but there's a Jinn that's mad as hell that we got away and he's on his way here to get this particular ring. If he does there's no telling what kind of powers he will have and not too mention you'll never see your son's soul again." It was enough to shut him up. It was enough to shut everyone up. Haadiya was one tough chick. I think she was shocked at the response she gotten from the group. Antonio held back a smile. Anthony gritted his teeth and decided to listen to what she had to say.

"First Courtney, you need to give the ring to Antonio."

"Wait why me! I don't want to get sucked into the ring!" Antonio protested.

Haadiya explained, "We are going to need your powers as well as Andrew's to do this."

Courtney tried to take the ring off. It wouldn't budge. "I can't get it off."

Haadiya thought it over, "Hmmm."

Courtney pulled and pulled. "Andrew..." She pleaded.

"I'm not doing anything."

"I think he may be holding on to you," Haadiya thought.

"No I'm not."

Courtney continued to struggle tugging at the ring. "Andrew let go then."

"I'm not holding on!"

"From what I read in the first book he wrote, he had some feelings that really didn't have closure," Haadiya analyzed, "Perhaps this is keeping him holding on to you." I didn't appreciate getting a psychological diagnosis by some obsessive book clubber.

"Will you excuse me for a moment?" Courtney went into the bathroom and started running water over her hand. She looked in the reflection and saw me staring back.

"Is it loosening up?" I asked as Courtney doused her hand under the blasting water.

She turned off the water, sighed, and looked at me dead in the eyes in the mirror. "Andrew, what's going on between you and me?"

"I don't know what you're talking about,"

I denied.

"Do you have feelings for me, Andrew?" Courtney asked in a frustrated manner. I felt offended for some reason. I threw the question back at her. She gave me the look as if I was being childish and maybe I was. Why did she even have to ask? Why couldn't I just be honest about it? What was it that I couldn't let go of?

"Andrew please! We don't have a lot of time!"

"What do you want me say Courtney? Yes! Yes, I like you. I like too much! There! Does that make it better? I'm crazy jealous that you haven't even given me a chance or a second thought and then you go and start dating Leonard. What did I do to you that was so wrong? Why can't you feel for me the way I feel for you?"

Courtney was shocked by the emotion that overtook me. I knew she could feel it. "I don't know what to say."

We stood in silence for a moment. She didn't even look at me in my eyes anymore. I felt a distance. That was enough for me. Not knowing what to say after I put my feelings on the line was enough. Here, she wanted to know how I felt and when I did, she left me with nothing.

"Andrew, I don't want to hurt you. You know all I want is to live a normal life and all this craziness makes me so unsure sometimes. It just doesn't seem real. I mean...I can't live life like this every day. I don't want to be the one to hurt you..."

But she was hurting me. Her rejection of me hurt. She was blabbering but I wasn't hearing her. I knew what she meant. You can't inhabit a person's soul without knowing what they mean. My life was too overwhelming for her. She couldn't handle the cards that God had dealt me.

She knew that by hanging around me she agreed to play the game as well and she wasn't sure if she liked the game of life that I was playing. That was her choice.

I was mad, but I was tired. I had spent over a year and half wishing and wanting and this is all she could say. Yeah, I was holding on; holding on to someone who didn't want to hold on to me.

"I'm sorry," she said.

"No, no...I'm sorry. Haadiya is right. I need to...I should've let go a long time ago." There was pain in my heart to even say the words because I knew that I needed to. If I didn't we wouldn't be able to fight what lied ahead. *"I'm letting you go, Courtney. Go ahead and live your life."*

Clunk! The ring fell off her finger easily and rolled in the basin of the sink. Courtney felt a cold disconnection. The ring sat in the sink and she looked in the mirror, but all she could see was herself.

CHAPTER FIFTY

The lights flickered on and off. Haadiya looked up and around trying to get to see if she could sense something. "We don't have much time. Do you understand what you have to do Antonio?" Haadiya told him. Courtney came back to join everyone just at that moment.

"Yeah I understand but I don't like it," Antonio responded.

"But if it will get Andrew free, then it must be done," Haadiya answered, "Courtney let Antonio wear the ring."

Courtney looked at Haadiya. "I hope you know what you're doing." There was a clash in the hallway.

"Now! Do it now! He's here!" Haadiya exclaimed and she pulled out an old book with ancient sigils written on it from her backpack.

Antonio took the ring. "You guys gonna be alright?"

Courtney nodded and Anthony put his hand on his son's shoulder. "Go." For a moment Antonio felt a sense of approval from his father. He didn't say anything about it. Antonio slipped on the ring and immediately felt this surge of power. That surge automatically used his powers to send him to the nether region dimension. He hadn't even tried to but it was almost instantaneous.

He took a breath and looked around. Andrew? I saw my brother. He had pulled me into the world with him. "What are we doing here?" I asked.

We moving between seconds. Courtney, Mack, Dad, and Haadiya appeared frozen in time. It was cold in this world yet there was no wind. I in particular felt very uncomfortable because I was a spirit out of my own body and here. It was like being exposed with no clothes and very vulnerable to whatever may decide to come my way.

"Quick, we have to figure a way to find mom."

"Mom?" I asked, "that's the plan? We came to the spirit realm to find mom?" This was getting crazy. I wasn't sure how mom was going to fit in the grand scheme of things.

"She can't come out of this realm unless something or someone brings her out and we're going to do just that."

Haadiya looked around. "It worked."

"Where'd they go?" Anthony said shocked to see his son use his power.

"One of Antonio's powers is to transcend the boundary of time," Courtney said.

Haadiya added, "Like many spirits entities can do. That's why we can't see them and they move so fast is because they can jump in these portals and move from place to place."

"Man I wish I had some powers," Mack once again expressed.

"I thought we already granted that wish before Mack." Ibo walked into the room so calmly and looked at everyone in the room as if he were just another part of the family.

Haadiya took a fighting stance and Courtney guarded over Mack. Anthony jumped next to Haadiya and grabbed a small chair much like a circus performer would do to fend off a lion.

"Let's all calm down. You know what I want." Ibo looked at Courtney. "Where's the ring?"

"We don't have it." Haadiya flipped through her book and said something in Arabic. It seemed to upset Ibo in some manner and he stepped back some.

"Speaking the holy names of God," he mumbled. He smiled at her cleverness. "You little girl are wise beyond your years." He looked her in her eyes and searched for her name and smiled when it was revealed "Haadiya. Yours is an old soul I see." Haadiya frowned in response.

"We don't have much time," I sensed, "Ibo is already catching on." I pulled my brother from the hospital room into the hallway, "How exactly are we supposed to find her?"

"I'm not sure." Antonio replied trying to think of an idea from the little he knew spiritually. "Ya think they would know?" He pointed down the hall and these slimy, leech like creatures attached themselves to the ceiling of the hospital.

"Some kind of demon I suppose," I observed. I was more intrigued than scared and I wondered what other spiritual beings simply lived amongst us that we couldn't see. Antonio

wasn't as interested and backed up some more. But as we looked around little spirits peppered the hallways and corners everywhere. Some appeared small as bugs while others were quite large and grotesque absorbing the life force from sick people like parasites. These beings were everywhere.

"*Oh that's gross. Next time I'm sick make sure you are praying over me,*" *Antonio said.*

"*Yeah Bro, will do, now that I see these things.*" *One of the worm-like creatures whipped out a sticky tongue to attach to us and I moved out the way.* "*They don't seem very friendly.*" *Another one grabbed my ankle and pulled me several feet down the hall.* "*Antonio!*" *I screamed reaching out for my twin.*

He ran after me. "*Don't worry Andrew I gotcha!*" *He grabbed my hand and slid along with me down the hall and up into the air as the worm-like demon wrapped around me like spaghetti. Antonio ripped at it's tentacles with his hands. But they kept regenerating; one became two, then they became four, growing a new one for every wound that Antonio inflicted.*

"It's growing itself back!" Antonio screamed. I didn't know what I could do. I didn't have a power that could battle this and I could feel the demon draining me of my power. I was getting more and more tired of struggling against the thing. I was simply being drained of my life force completely. The demon was killing me.

"No!" Antonio yelled, "Andrew hold on!" He slammed his fist into the creature, then out of no where a blast of light. The creature shriveled and shrieked and released its grip of both me and my brother.

We dropped to the floor unharmed except for a few bruises. I regained my focus to see where and what had given off the light and a shadowy figure materialized holding some sort of orb.

"Andy?"

I looked and squinted my eyes. The voice was all too familiar. "Mom?" I pulled myself to my feet. Antonio looked up in shock. This would be his first time to see her.

She ran up to us both and examined me with her eyes "What has happened to you? Why are you out of your body? Didn't I tell you not use your powers to seek me?" She was being a mother as usual.

"How did you stop that thing?"

"That's a siphon demon, I used the residual positive energy of people in the physical plane; prayers, compliments, etc. a little of that goes a long way when you pack it together like a snow ball, makes a good weapon against demons. But that doesn't tell me why you are

here."

"Mom, we're all in trouble, and technically I didn't use my powers, Antonio did." Antonio was still in the same spot, stunned.

Mom looked at him and held her peace for a second to compose herself. There was her other baby that she had given up. She stepped forward. "Antonio."

"Uh, hi." He gave a small smile and it was the first time I saw him be somewhat shy. She had no words to express her love for him.

"You look good," She said, "I'm sure you have so many questions."

Antonio looked up and around and found eye contact with me, "Uh, I guess, but I'm not here for me. We have to get Andrew back into his body before something bad happens. You see we got a hold of King Solomon's ring and we were tricked by a…"

"A jinn," Mom completed his sentence,

"yes I know all about them. Tricky little devils aren't they? So," she looked at me, *"you are trapped in the ring and where is this jinn?"*

"He is looking for the ring."

"If he gets a hold of the ring then he will be too powerful. So you need some other spirit to inhabit the ring to take Andrew's place." She was putting two and two together quickly and Antonio hadn't said a word. I thought it was perhaps her power she was using but then again it could've been her mother's intuition. She looked at me with warm eyes and tried to hold back tears that would not form from a mother who was just a spirit.

"It is a mother's job to protect her children." She looked back at Antonio. *"I love my boys, I always have."* Antonio put his head down to not show his emotion. I could feel the intensity of what he was feeling in spades. His love for her was overwhelming.

"There's just one catch." Mom said, *I don't have a body anymore and in order for a spirit to command the ring for any manner of time they have to have a body.*

"We know of one body that is available for rent," Antonio said. Suddenly, a whirlwind portal formed in the middle of the hallway. Smaller demons were blown all over from the vortex.

"What is that?" Mom yelled.

My face went pale and I felt my heart drop. "It's Ibo."

"Where is the ring!" he screamed entering into the realm.

Antonio grabbed Mom's hand and ran down the hall. I blast a force field in between us and Ibo that engulfed the hallway like a plastic bubble to buy us some time. I followed quickly after Antonio.

We made it to our destination. We were

in Tonya's room.

"Mom," Antonio said, "you have to possess her body and when you do I will pass the ring to you."

"I get it," Mom said, "then I will free Andrew." *She smiled my way. "But after the ring takes possession of me, what will you do?"*

"We have to get Ibo back in the ring."

"And how exactly were you going to do that my son?" My mom sarcastically asked.

"We haven't exactly gotten that far yet," Antonio admitted.

"Don't worry I will handle this." She held Antonio's hand as he led the way from the spirit realm into ….

…the physical one in a flash of light. He appeared to arrive alone. But he could feel the presence of both me and mom around him. A cold wind whirled inside the room where Tonya was on life support and then her chest jumped up and the heart monitor sped up. Her hand gripped the bed and she wheezed.

"Mom!" Antonio yelled. Dad and Haadiya came running from down the hall.

"Ibo suddenly disappeared," Haadiya said, "did you find your mother okay?"

"Yeah, that part of the plan is done," Antonio said.

"Boys," A weak voice from the bed said.

"She's awake." Antonio ran over to the side of the bed. It was weird looking at Tonya and looking in her eyes he could definitely see somebody different.

"I've never done this before. It's quite awkward but this Tonya girl is practically gone. Why do they still have her on life support? Even I'm having a hard time keeping this body from dying," she said weakly trying to sit up.

"Maybe this will help," Antonio said placing the ring on her finger. A surge of energy flowed through her body. She jerked and curled back. Her neck stretched as if she were being shocked.

Her eyes popped open and she sat up. "That's much better."

"Andrea?" Anthony stood in the door. He wanted to be sure that was really her. She got out of the bed and put a robe on. "Anthony…" In Tonya's body she was still about the same height as she was in her own life and she situated the hair that Tonya had in the way she would normally pull her own hair back. "It's me, don't worry. Thank you, for taking good care of the boys."

"I'm not doing that well," he criticized himself.

"Don't be so hard on yourself, Hun." She patted his chest and tightened her robe. "We're not exactly the normal family."

Ibo teleported into the room. "I'm really

getting tired of this wild goose chase. Why don't you all stop running and give me what I want!" He flicked his hand and blasted a force that knocked everyone to the floor.

Everyone had the wind knocked out them except for Mom. She stood back to her feet in full power and energized for a fight. She was using her amplified power and mine as well. It was like I was seeing life through her eyes. "No one and I mean no one…" She fixed her pony tail. "messes with my family." She dusted herself off.

"And who may I ask are you?"

"Someone who's heaven sent!" Andrea dropped kicked him in the chest. Ibo flew back into the hallway. Courtney peeked out of Mack's room and gasped.

"Tonya?"

"No, babygirl, it's Andrew's mom, go back inside while I handle this," She said not missing a beat to punch Ibo again.

Courtney went back inside Mack's room and closed the door.

CHAPTER FIFTY ONE

"What's going on out there?" Mack asked. Courtney was backed up against the door.

"You don't want to know. Evidently, Haadiya's plan worked. They managed to find Andrea's spirit," Courtney explained.

"Man if this aint something out of some crazy movie," Mack laughed to himself.

"Tell me about it." Courtney didn't seem to be so calm about it, "I think we'll be safe in here."

"Hey…" Mack reassured, "It's gonna work out. Andrew and Antonio are two forces to be reckoned with and with their mom's awakened spirit I'm sure that adds to it. This is some kind of family!"

"I'm glad you're so excited," Courtney said listening to the door. She could hear banging and clanging against the wall. A woman was yelling and making loud declarations which Courtney assumed to be Andrea.

"Sounds like she's winning."

"Yeah his mom is something else. She's a pretty strong valiant woman. They say guys go after girls that remind them of their mother," Mack imposed.

Courtney stopped eavesdropping for a moment to look his way. "What do you mean by that?"

Mack smiled. "Courtney, come on. I was in the ring with Andrew. I was feeling what he felt as well as what you felt. I know."

"You know what?"

"I know that you love him as much as he loves you," Mack proclaimed, "Why are you guys making this so hard on yourselves?"

"I don't think we should be talking about this right now Mack, there's a crazy jinn in the hall."

Mack shook his head. "Courtney you can't stop living and loving because of problems. Problems will always be there. And if you're waiting for all that to end then you're just waiting to love someone after you die and then what's the point?" He sat up in the bed. "I know you just think, it's just crazy ol' Mack talking out his head but being stuck in that ring gives a man time to think." He giggled at the thought. "You guys have a special bond that you don't find too often. You should try to see where that goes. It's that love that energizes you and strengthens you. It's that unified love that brings you one step closer to who God is. And with that love, no devil in this world can stop you." Mack smiled.

Courtney was amazed at this profound

wisdom. "Wow Mack, that was…beautiful."

"Yeah, I should write greeting cards huh?" He joked. "But naw fa real…you two are trippin.'" Mack kept it real.

Courtney whined, "Mack you don't understand. It's complicated. I'm with Leonard now, and I have a commitment."

"Damn, Courtney, don't miss out on a good thing. Guys like Andrew come once in a lifetime. That's my boy, and I would love to see him find the love that he truly deserves."

She smiled. "Mack, thank you." She walked away from the door, sat on his bed and touched his hand. "I appreciate that."

The door burst open as a girl was hurled through it and slammed against the wall. Courtney screamed. Ibo stood in the doorway breathing hard.

Mack grabbed Courtney's arm. "Oh shit."

CHAPTER FIFTY TWO

When Courtney had closed the door, my mother had begun wreaking havoc on Ibo. She ran up on him with supernatural speed and slammed fist after fist into his face not given the jinn time to dematerialize from his physical form. When he did and reappeared behind her, she anticipated it and back kicked him in the abdomen and flung across the hall.

The ruckus caused the nurse and other security officers to run into the hall. Andrea simple raised her hand. "Sleep." And they all passed out in the hallway.

"You're no normal human," Ibo said getting up, "who are you?"

"I'm a mad black woman and you…" She ran up on Ibo. "are gonna learn not to hurt my babies!" She upper-cutted him. Ibo vapored away and reformed holding his chin. He grabbed her throat and slammed her against the wall.

Staring her in the eyes he was about one inch from her face, "You are…Donyel's offspring," he snarled now realizing what he was up against, "You are of the Nephilim; no wonder." She pushed against him with her legs and flung him, once again back.

"Get your hands off me!" She fixed her robe.

Antonio ran out in the hall. "Mom!"

"Go back in the room, Antonio!" she yelled. For the second she was distracted Ibo teleported with a quickness and sucker punched her, flinging her across the hall, through the door in the next room.

Courtney screamed. Being a mortal body was taking its toil on Andrea and be that Tonya's body had already gone through some turmoil she was beginning to bleed and lose strength.

"A spirit is nothing without a body to exist in. I will send you back to the third heaven where you belong," Ibo said.

"You first," Andrea said wiping the blood from her mouth. Ibo tore the door from its' hinges and lifted it above his head.

"No!" Courtney screamed as Ibo slammed down with full force. But all it hit was my field surrounding my mother. I was protecting her.

"Don't worry mom, I'm here with you," I said protecting her with my power. It was just enough time for her get her senses back.

Ibo looked at Mack and Courtney. "You can protect yourself but you can't protect them." He laughed and swung the door their direction.

"No!" someone said it. I wasn't sure. All I knew was everything stopped. Ibo was frozen. Over by the bed, Courtney clung Mack in fear and the steel hospital door was just inches from striking them. *Antonio was next to me breathing hard trying to get his mind together. Once again he had pulled himself, me and mom in between time.*

"What are we going to do?" Antonio asked.

"Quickly, before he realizes what we're doing and joins us here," Mom said. I saw her spirit pull away from Tonya's body but she still had the ring and with the jewel part she touched it to Ibo's forehead.

"By the power of the Father of gods and lords I banish you jinn!" she said. Ibo began screaming, unfrozen from time and awakening in the realm where we were.

He began to dematerialize into a whirlpool of little balls of light like fireflies buzzing around quickly. Those little orbs were soon sucked into the ring itself and Ibo once again was one with the ring.

She fell to the floor in relief "I got him," Andrea said. Antonio moved the door that was directed at Courtney. I sat on the floor and hugged my mother and she hugged me back. "Where'd you learn to do that?" I asked.

"You learn a lot fighting demons in the netherworld." She looked over and saw Antonio just watching and she held her hand out. He took it and joined in the hug.

"But I couldn't have done it without my precious babies."

CHAPTER FIFTY THREE

Mom resituated herself back into the hospital bed. "It's time for me to go now. I think I've done enough damage." Antonio knelt beside the bed. His eyes were wet. "Hey, hey...don't cry," she said, "You know I am so proud of you."

"I just wish I had more time with you; that's all," Antonio said. All were silent. Anthony sat in the corner of the dark hospital room watching the whole thing. Courtney was holding up Mack in the doorway who decided to say their goodbyes as well. Haadiya was in the hall waiting.

"Antonio, I know this is hard for you baby. But I want you to be strong. I'm sorry we kept so much from you. I'm sorry I kept….myself from you. But know that we just wanted to protect you. That's all parents want to do." She laughed, "But it looks like you two ended up protecting us instead." She looked at Anthony. He walked over and sat on the bed.

"I never really got to say goodbye," Anthony said.

"I know," Andrea smiled back, "I've never really been the type that was good at saying goodbye."

"Yeah, you were always a little stubborn." He patted Antonio's head.

"I will always love you Andrea," Anthony said holding her hand.

"I love you," Andrea said, "But it's time for you to let go." And she pulled her hand away. "I sense some things for you, Anthony. You're still living. Don't close yourself off to love especially in the name of God. God is love."

"What are you talking about, I'm not

closed to…"

"Anthony," Andrea said gently, "just for once, open your eyes." It was a suggestion. She was seeing into his soul and knowing exactly what was up. She saw things in him that he didn't want to see in himself.

"When I release Andrew from the ring, I will be the primary spirit of the ring. I will be here with Ibo. Take the ring and dispose of it."

"What will happen to you?" Antonio said.

"Don't worry about me, Tonio," she said. "I'm a spirit, I'll be okay. Spirits don't die. And being in the ring is whole lot better than being trapped in the third realm. There's a lot more to the spirit realm than we know. Perhaps there's a way for me get free, until then..." She smiled.

"Perhaps," Anthony said with tears in his eyes, and he kissed her, "Goodbye."

She smiled at the unexpected kiss. "Take

care and Merry Christmas." She held her hand in the air. "Andrew…I release you."

CHAPTER FIFTY FOUR

"Man somebody stole my car and you know what! They found it in the river! Some Christmas this has been!" Leonard yelled on the phone. Courtney tried to console him.

"Hey Leo, can I call you back?" Courtney asked. I was just getting up from a very long sleep out of bed. The whole house smelled of food which was an awesome smell. Just being able to smell, you never know how great that is until you've left your body. My body ached and I was stiff all over. The least they could've done was rotate me a little.

"How do you feel?" she asked concerned.

"Better." I smiled, "How's Mack?"

"He's back home, Sophie called and was all excited saying how God had given her a

Christmas miracle."

I laughed. "We're like God's secret agents aren't we?"

"Yeah, we're something like that." She shook her head and helped me find a seat on the couch.

"Welcome back to the land of the living. You hungry?" Karen asked from the kitchen.

"Yes ma'am." I looked in the room. Haadiya was sitting at the kitchen table drinking some tea.

"So I finally get to meet you in the flesh, Mr. Turner." She stood up.

"Yep." I shook her hand. "Thank you, Haadiya, I mean you just came out of no where but thanks for helping us out."

"You still have some explaining to do," Courtney said.

"I'm waiting as well." Anthony walked from the his self made library room.

Jason and Antonio came from outside. "Look who is finally awake, Rip Van Winkle!" Antonio joked. He grabbed my head like a basketball and shook it.

"Aye Man! Quit!" I was still stiff and that didn't feel good. "Now that everyone's here, Haadiya, fess up. Who are you? Why do you know so much about us and spirits at such a young age?"

Antonio looked at her. "Are we unwrapping secrets or unwrapping gifts today?" He was impatient.

"Please," I gave Haadiya the floor, "Share with us. You have our undivided attention."

She seemed somewhat hesitant. "Well, um." She stood up and I could see the little girl in the warrior now, "If I tell you the truth you probably won't believe me."

"Trust me, there's nothing you can say

that will surprise us," Karen commented and sat at the table.

Haadiya grinned and stuck her hands in her pocket. "I was sent for several reasons," she began.

"Andrew, we need your help."

"My help?" I asked, "wait, who is we?"

"We are a secret sect of…demon hunters."

Karen almost choked on her tea. "Okay now I've heard every thing." She went back to the sink. "Lord help us."

Haadiya continued. "Demons need bodies to exist in this world or at least to do damage. We hunt down some of the major demon lords that have possessed people and banish them. Once they are banished usually it frees up the souls of so many people that are being possessed by minor demons."

I was trying to understand. "So you need

my help in these demon hunts?"

"No we have that pretty down packed," She said proudly.

"One of our own has gone rebel. She was the one who trained me and took me under her wing when my own mother was killed by demons." I felt sympathy for Haadiya.

"She was the one who told me about you and your family. The problem is after her own husband was killed she lost it. Now we can't find her and instead of hunting the demons and banishing them from people. She is simply…" She paused.

"What?" I asked.

"She's hunting them down and killing them."

I tried to process what I was hearing. "So wait…this teacher of yours is hunting demon possessed people and killing them off."

"But I mean these people are really doing

major evil in the world, and if you knew what they did you would understand but it's just that…well, we were never killing the bodies to rid of the demons. Simply trapping them and exorcising the demons. But as you can very well see that takes a while to do. I guess she lost patience and decided to take matters in her own hands. Our second in command thought it'd be best for me to find you because of my relation to you to get your assistance."

"Wait, assistance in what? " Anthony interjected, "In chasing down your demon huntress serial killer? I don't think I want my son involved."

"But, you're already involved."

"How so?" Courtney asked.

"My teacher is someone you know." She looked at my dad.

Anthony looked suspicious. "And who exactly could that be?"

"Years ago, did you meet a girl in college named Valerie Larue, Mack's aunt, and your old college friend?" She asked.

"Valerie?" Karen was shocked, "all these years."

"Oh man." I felt a pain in my stomach, this was getting deeper and deeper by the second, then I thought over what she said, "you mentioned that you'd be best to come here because of your relation to us. What relation is that?"

She gulped in slight nervousness. "Um, I've been the one calling all this time." She looked at Anthony. "Because…"

Everyone was silent.

"I'm your daughter."

Everyone was still silent.

Anthony's mouth dropped.

Antonio leaned over to me and whispered, "See I told you Dad wasn't all that innocent."

CHAPTER FIFTY FIVE

The cold Christmas night wind blows against the screen door causing it to slam. SLAM! SLAM! It's enough to wake the old preacher from his sleep. Pastor Francis, the widower husband of Maggie, Andrea Turner's biological mother. His connection is something he'd rather forget. A nightmare that won't stop haunting him. A howling in the wind that forever keeps him up at night.

Pastor Francis finally goes to the front door to secure the screen. He pulls his robe closer to himself as he tries to grab the flapping screen.

"Thomas," A whisper in the wind says. Thomas Francis looks out into the darkness, grumbles and prepares to close the door.

"Merry Christmas, Thomasss," his name is hissed like a serpent.

Pastor Francis jumps, startled at the tall pale white man with flowing black hair behind him. Pastor Francis runs down the steps but stumbles into the grass. Donyel hovers over as the moonlight creates a frightening affect on his face. Besides, as an angel, Donyel can choose to look as beautiful or hideous as he wills. And this time Donyel chooses to have fun.

"It's been too long Thomas!!!" Donyel cackles.

"No! No! Devil be gone!" Thomas grabs his chest, "Devil be…" his voice chokes. "gone." Thomas jerks in pain and passes out. The old man's heart couldn't take it.

Donyel leans over and holds Thomas like *Michelangelo's Pieta.* "Father God accept this soul into your kingdom," he mocks, "his blood be not on my hands." And it isn't. Pastor

Francis's fear is what killed Pastor Francis. And as Donyel lays Pastor Thomas to rest in some secret place in the forest, Donyel returns to Pastor Francis's home, in Pastor Francis's robe and with wave of his hand. Donyel shape shifts to look like Pastor Thomas Francis.

CHAPTER FIFTY SIX

"How was your Christmas?" Amelia asked. She sat in my apartment on my couch as I tried to journal all that happened. I laughed because I knew I couldn't tell her the truth.

"It was like any other Christmas I guess; family, meeting up with old family, and the drama that comes from that."

"Yeah, I've been there before." She said rubbing my shoulders, "Hey here's your present." Amelia was all too good to me and yet I felt as if I didn't deserve such goodness in my life.

"I didn't get you anything. I got caught up in the drama with my family. I'm sorry." I don't know how I could've let something so important slip my mind.

She smiled. "It's okay. Open mine anyway."

I unwrapped the small package. Only jewelry came such small boxes; or severed pinkies, but Amelia didn't look like the prankster type. I opened the lid and inside was a small oval locket.

"You can place a picture of anyone you like," she said.

I thought it over but it didn't take long, "Thank you, would you mind if I put a picture of my mother in here?"

Amelia hugged my neck and kissed my cheek. "I think that would be perfect." Amelia was a good woman. I went back to writing my journal.

After my mother was taken possession by the ring Anthony was given responsibility over it by Shariel to hide it in a special place. The ring could be dangerous in the hands of a demon or angel. Anthony took on the responsibility with honor. Courtney went back to California with Leonard. And somehow I have to just deal with the fact that she is with someone. Besides I have someone in my life as well. It's just that I haven't told Amelia all my secrets yet.

I wasn't sure how she would react to knowing what I and even my family was all about. Would it be too much for her? I wasn't ready to find out, yet. I was just enjoying the moment. But sooner or later I would have to tell her. Speaking of family, I had to admit Haadiya letting the cat out the bag that she is our half sister surprised me probably more than the demon hunter thing. And while I'm interested in finding out more on what she wants me to do, I still think there are more secrets to Haadiya. Antonio is yet trying to find his own identity outside all of this. I know that somehow he will find out his own personal meaning in all this craziness. My dad and Karen, who knows what may happen with them; Anthony has issues letting go; I now see where I get it from. I haven't even told Mack about his aunt being this rebel demon hunter, but I know I'll need him through all of this. And when it comes to Donyel, it still bothers me that he's out there, somewhere. But where? Only time will tell, because Donyel is the type to never just attack like a wild dog. Whatever he does is planned out and methodical. And I, just have to be ready….for whatever comes next.

COMING SOON by Montré Bible

THE SONS OF HEAVEN

Book V of the Heaven Sent Series

Preview:

"Indigo. But folks around here call me Indi."

"Like Indie Arie" I smiled and she smiled back. I felt a good vibe when I shook her hand. I reminded myself that I had a girlfriend. But there's nothing wrong with looking.

"Indi's great grandmother was Nephilim as well," Haadiya informed me.

"You too, but how?"

"You don't think you're the only one do you?" She smiled in amazement at my lack of knowing,

"I have the ability to see demons. That's why I'm here. I can see the differences in people's eyes when they are possessed but I can also see the essence of them when they move around."

I grew even more interested,. "Really? Wow that's interesting. I've seen like shadows and things and sometimes I hear voices."

"Well I'm not quite like that." She smiled. "it's only if they move. It's sorta like watching a chameleon move around and you finally spot it." This blew my mind to find someone who understood somewhat my experience and that made me more comfortable.

"You guys will have to talk later." Haadiya took my hand and directed me to the stair case, "right now Andrew needs to meet Lincoln."

Montré Bible   Heaven's Power

Made in the USA
Lexington, KY
18 January 2015